Catherine MacPhail says:

As a writer, I'm always on the look out for characters and incidents that might spark off ideas for a book, and I have a notebook full of stories about the funny old men I have come across. Like the one who kept his hearing aid in his pocket and his daughter had to follow him around, bent double, so she could talk into the pocket and he could hear her.

When I went into schools I would tell the children these stories. I would then go into my 'what if' mode. What if this old man was your grandfather? And what if he was driving you up the wall? From there I would do workshops based around the Granda stories. The children loved them, and always asked me if I was going to write a book about Granda. And suddenly I thought – why not? So I did. And this is it.

Catherine MacPhail has won the Kathleen Fidler Award, the Verghereto Award in Italy, and one of the first Scottish Children's Book Awards. As well as her children's books, she also writes for the radio, and has had two situation comedy series on BBC Radio 2. Catherine lives in Greenock, Scotland.

Books by Catherine MacPhail

CATCH US IF YOU CAN
TRIBES
WHEELS

Catch Us If You Can

CATHERINE MACPHAIL

PUFFIN

PUFFIN BOOKS

Published by the Penguin Group
Penguin Books Ltd, 80 Strand, London WC2R 0RL, England
Penguin Group (USA), Inc., 375 Hudson Street, New York, New York 10014, USA
Penguin Books Australia Ltd, 250 Camberwell Road, Camberwell, Victoria 3124, Australia
Penguin Books Canada Ltd, 10 Alcorn Avenue, Toronto, Ontario, Canada M4V 3B2
Penguin Books India (P) Ltd, 11 Community Centre, Panchsheel Park, New Delhi – 110 017, India
Penguin Books (NZ) Ltd, Cnr Rosedale and Airborne Roads, Albany, Auckland, New Zealand
Penguin Books (South Africa) (Pty) Ltd, 24 Sturdee Avenue,
Rosebank 2196, South Africa

Penguin Books Ltd, Registered Offices: 80 Strand, London WC2R 0RL, England

www.penguin.com

First published 2004
2

Set in 13/15pt Baskerville MT by Palimpsest Book Production Limited, Polmont, Stirlingshire
Made and printed in England by Clays Ltd, St Ives plc

British Library Cataloguing in Publication Data
A CIP catalogue record for this book is available from the British Library

ISBN 0-141-31702-7

For Katie and Danny
With love

'Where have you been, Granda? We'll be getting called any minute.'

My granda shuffled into the doctor's waiting room, rubbing his hands together.

'Wee puff of my pipe, Rory, my boy,' he said. 'You know how nervous I get going in to see this doctor.'

'He's only going to give you more pills and tell you to stop smoking.'

'He's a moaning old devil, that doctor. That's the only enjoyment I've got left. He's got me on heart pills, head pills, pills to make me go to the toilet, pills to stop me going to the toilet. It's no wonder I forget to take them.'

I didn't even bother answering him. My granda never forgot to take his pills, because I made sure he took them. Sometimes, living with my granda was like having a baby in the house.

He couldn't keep still and started wandering over to the noticeboard. 'Come here and see this, Rory,' he said, beckoning me to him. 'Could I apply for this? It's extra money.'

The old woman sitting beside the noticeboard tutted when he said that. I didn't blame her.

'You've got to be pregnant to get it, Granda.'

That made him laugh. 'Hardly likely at my age, eh, son?'

I pulled him back to our seats. 'Now sit down, Granda, and behave yourself.'

He managed it for about two minutes . . . until a young girl came struggling in with a baby in her arms. There he was, always the gentleman, on his feet again, holding the door open for her.

'In you come, darlin',' he said to her. 'Rory, get the lady's bag. That's my boy.'

The 'lady', who only looked about sixteen, smiled and thanked him and took a seat. Granda didn't. Now he was up, he stayed up, and he couldn't resist babies. He bent right down to the smiling baby and started talking.

'You are a bonny little thing. Now what's your name?'

He could be so embarrassing. What's your name, indeed! As if the baby could tell him. She only giggled and dribbled. A bit like my granda really.

'Her name's Lorelei,' the girl said, in an adenoidal voice.

'Lorelei? That's a lovely name. That was Marilyn Monroe's name in one of her pictures. Did you know that?'

If there was one thing my granda knew all about, it was films. A fount of useless information I was always telling him. Marilyn Monroe was one of his big favourites. 'Did you call her after Marilyn Monroe?' he asked.

The girl looked baffled. 'She's not called Marilyn. She's called Lorelei.'

The woman who was sitting near the noticeboard suddenly started sniffing. 'Is that smoke I smell?'

The girl was suddenly alert. 'I smell it as well.' Her eyes went wide as saucers. 'You're on fire.' She jumped to her feet, away from my granda, pointing in panic. 'You're on fire!'

She didn't have to say it twice. Everybody in the waiting room could see he was on fire. At least, his pocket was. Smoke was belching out and Granda was twisting himself round to see. Before I could run to him the smoke alarm began to wail. The receptionist was racing towards us, screaming: 'Right. Who's smoking!'

Granda was still laughing. 'What's the problem?' he asked calmly.

'You're the problem!' I yelled. I grabbed the vase filled with flowers from the receptionist's desk and threw the water all over him. He certainly wasn't calm after that.

Dr Nicol leaned back and studied my granda carefully. 'Are you all dried out now, Mister McIntosh?'

My granda still wasn't talking to me. 'No, thanks to this boy here. He practically drowned me.'

'You were on fire, Granda. I put you out.'

It hadn't been the first time either. I had lost count of the times my granda had set something on fire with that pipe of his. He never put it out properly.

He always left it to smoulder, until finally, whoof! It would burst into flame again.

'If I catch double pneumonia, it'll be all your fault.' (He pronounced it 'p-eumonia'. He always did.)

Dr Nicol was smiling. He had been our doctor ever since I could remember; had been the family doctor since before I was born.

Family doctor. There was only Granda and me. Were the two of us enough to make a family? I suppose we were.

Dr Nicol liked us. He said we were like a double act, me and my granda. He said we always made him laugh. Huh, Dr Nicol didn't have to live with him.

'OK, now, Rory, you have all your granda's prescriptions?'

I held them up to show him that I had, then I folded them carefully and put them in my pocket.

'And has he been taking his pills regularly?'

'I make sure he does, doctor.'

The doctor spoke to my granda. 'You're a lucky man to have a grandson like this, Mister McIntosh.'

My granda only shrugged. 'I moulded him into the boy he is today. He owes me everything. And what thanks do I get? He tries to drown me.'

But I knew, deep down, my granda did appreciate me. He told me so lots of times. Especially as he slipped off to sleep.

'You're a great boy, Rory,' he would say. ' I don't deserve ye.'

Dr Nicol leaned forward. 'I'm going to do my best to get you a home help.'

My granda began to protest at that. 'We don't need anybody, do we, son?'

The doctor didn't give me a chance to answer. 'Rory can't do everything. He does the shopping and the cooking. He cleans the house. He's only a boy, Mister McIntosh. He needs help.'

My granda looked at me. 'I'm a good help, so I am, son?'

'You're brilliant, Granda,' I said loyally. But to tell the truth, I thought a home help would be a great idea. Then I wouldn't have to worry about my granda so much.

'How's his memory these days, Rory?' Dr Nicol held me back as my granda shuffled out of his office.

'Well, I found his shoes in the fridge and the milk at the bottom of the wardrobe this morning, but other than that, he's fine.'

Dr Nicol nodded. 'Phone me if you need me, Rory.' And, as I ran to catch up with my granda, I had no idea he was already on the phone himself.

2

'OK, Granda, I left my homework jotter on the table. Where did you put it?'

My granda was still shuffling about in his pjs, munching his toast. 'I get the blame for everything in this place,' he said, spitting out toast everywhere. 'I probably put it in your school bag. Have you looked there?'

I hadn't. I assumed since my school rucksack was the most logical place to put it, that would be the last place he would think of. I prayed it was there. Mrs Foley, my teacher, had told me off three times already this week for forgetting my homework. Of course, I hadn't actually forgotten it once, it was simply that I couldn't find it. My granda was always putting it away 'somewhere safe' and then couldn't remember where.

He suddenly shouted from the kitchen. 'I remember now. I put it in your school bag when I was putting the rubbish down the chute.'

I went cold all over. He had rubbish in one hand and my homework in the other? No. Please. Not that. I had already spotted the bulge in my rucksack. It didn't look like any homework jotter to me.

I opened the flap and peeked inside. There it was.

Not my jotter, of course, but a bag of eggshells and potato peelings, all neatly tied up.

And my homework jotter? I could picture it now. Lying at the bottom of the rubbish chute, under a pile of Chinese takeaways, dirty nappies and empty tins.

'Did you get it?' My granda came hobbling down the hall. I held up the plastic bag.

'Oops,' he said.

'So, what excuse can I give old holy Foley?' I asked my classmates as we waited in the playground for the bell to ring. 'I can't say I've forgotten it again.'

Darren Fisher, my best pal, had a great idea. 'Tell her aliens took it. I saw that on the telly last night. Aliens captured this boy and when they brought him back he couldn't remember anything.'

'Used it.' I reminded him. 'I don't know why she didn't believe that one. Sounded perfectly logical to me.'

My classmates all had gathered round me, desperately trying to help. They loved my granda; thought his exploits were hilarious. They were always eager for more stories about him. Like the time he was almost arrested for shoplifting when a hanger with a suit on it got caught in the belt of his raincoat and he walked out of the shop with it attached to him.

Naturally, I always embellished these stories, trying to make them even funnier. Mind you, I didn't have to embellish them much with my granda.

7

But lately my granda's behaviour wasn't so much funny as worrying.

In the end, I told the truth . . . well, almost.

'I lost it, Mrs Foley. I'm really sorry.'

She raised one of her massive eyebrows. Honestly, you could go on safari in Mrs Foley's eyebrows. 'I almost believe that, Rory. It's so simple. No aliens. No dogs fighting over it. No seagulls flying past you and whipping it out of your hands.' She was referring to excuses I had used in the past. Pretty good ones too, I thought.

She bent closer to me. 'How is your grandfather these days?' It was very difficult not to notice that Mrs Foley also had a moustache. A thin line of dark hair just above her lip. She was one hairy woman.

'He's doing fine, Mrs Foley.'

'Is he coming along to Parents' Night?'

That got me angry. My granda never missed a Parents' Night. 'Of course he is.'

I should have remembered then that Mrs Foley might not know how conscientious my granda was. She had only started at the school this term. She hadn't had a Parents' Night so far.

'Good. Now, I'd like you to stay behind at lunchtime to do your homework.'

I shook my head. 'No can do, Mrs Foley.'

She frowned at me and her eyebrows collided.

'My granda makes my dinner,' I explained. 'He'll be waiting for me.'

I caught her watching me as I ran out of the

playground at lunchtime, checking if I was telling the truth. I could almost feel her eyes follow me down the road and across the street to our block of flats. Did she see me sneak into the bakers' at the corner for two hot pies? Did she know already that Granda never had my lunch ready? In fact, Granda relied on me to bring *him* his lunch every day. I *had* to go home at lunchtime. I had to make sure he was taking his pills.

Well, even if Mrs Foley did know, why should I care? My granda had taken care of me all my life. Now, when he was getting old and forgetful and was never quite well, now it was my turn to look after my granda.

3

'*F*ootball practice, Rory McIntosh.' Mr Hood stood in front of me barring my way. 'I've seen you in the playground. You're a good little footballer. You should be in the team.'

'Don't like football, sir,' I lied.

'You used to,' Mr Hood reminded me, as if I didn't know. 'You were in the team once.'

'I was a lot younger then, sir. I've changed.'

Darren guffawed. 'He's turning into a lassie, sir.'

When she heard that, Mary Bailey aimed a kick right at him. She didn't care that a teacher was standing in front of her. Darren let out a howl of pain. 'What do you mean, Darren Fisher? I'm the best football player in the school. And I'm a lassie.'

Darren jumped around holding his shin. 'I'm not too sure about that,' he dared to say and Mary kicked him again and called him a very rude name.

As Mr Hood dragged her off to the headmaster's office she shouted back at us: 'Wimp!' I don't know if she meant me or Darren.

'You should be on the team, Rory. They only put her in because you left.'

'And because she was going to sue the school if they didn't.' Darren had maybe forgotten that.

'Anyway, you know I can't get to football practice. How would I get to the games? Who would look after my granda?'

Darren rubbed his sore leg and mumbled, 'Do you not think your granda should maybe be in a . . . home or something?'

I nearly kicked him then. 'Don't you ever say that! My granda will never go into a home. It would kill him.'

How often had I heard my granda talking about Rachnadar, the local old people's hospital? Granda always told me that was where you went when nobody wanted you. 'Shoot me before you put me in there, son,' he would say. The very building, stuck on the edge of town, dark and forbidding, frightened him. It frightened me too.

'No way my granda's going into a home,' I said again.

Darren tried to make it sound better. 'It's not me that says that, Rory. I've heard my mum say —'

I didn't let him finish. 'You tell your mum to mind her own business.'

I ran off before Darren could say another word. It was almost as if at that moment I was afraid that someone – a parent, a teacher – would reach out and grab me, keep me from running home, put my granda into Rachnadar before I could stop them.

Never!

Why couldn't people realize that I was all my granda had and, even more terrifying to think about,

Granda was all I had too. If they put Granda into a home . . . where would I go?

With Parents' Night coming up soon I was trying to coach Granda on how to behave. He had just finished a big plate of egg and chips, and he wiped his mouth with the edge of his sleeve! Honestly, you couldn't take him anywhere.

'Don't do that in front of Mrs Foley. She's dead posh, you know.'

'Don't you worry about a thing, Rory, my boy. I'll charm the knickers off her.'

I almost choked on my chips. 'Don't say anything like that to her either. She's dead holy.'

Granda laughed loudly and his false teeth rattled in his mouth. 'Holy Foley!'

I'd been trying to coach him for over an hour now. I wanted him to reassure Mrs Foley that he had all his marbles.

It was going to be a struggle.

I had come home to discover that Granda had peeled a bag of apples and cut them into chips.

'Be honest,' he said. 'They look just like potatoes, and anyway what were they doing in the potato rack?'

'You put them there,' I told him. 'Remember? The same time you put the potatoes in the fruit bowl.'

That shut him up for about a second. 'Does that mean you don't want the apple pie?'

Over the last few days he'd been trying to help, trying to cook, but his efforts scared me. I'd told him over and over that I didn't want him cooking. It wasn't the first time that he'd left the electric ring switched on and burned out a pot.

As we sat that night watching television, my mind was on other things. I thought Granda was snoozing but instead he was watching me closely.

'What are you thinking about, son?' He leaned across to me.

'I'm wondering what my dad was like, Granda.'

I knew mentioning him would make him angry. It always did. He banged his fist on the edge of the table.

'He was a spoiled brat of a boy! I've told you a hundred times. I was too old to be a dad. I was forty-five when he was born. Too blinking old. I told your granny that. But she was that happy to have a baby. Never thought it would happen. She just loved that boy. We both spoiled him rotten. Anything he wanted he got, and when he got tired of it, he threw it aside. Toys when he was a boy and, when he grew up, he did the same thing with your mother.'

His voice softened. 'She was a lovely lassie.' He always said the same thing about my mother. No praise was too high for her – a young girl left alone with a baby when my dad upped and left her. 'He did it with you too. Couldn't face responsibility. It killed your poor mother. She was heartbroken.' He was getting angry again at the memory of it, far in the past, but still as raw as ever. 'When he left, Rory, I told him never to come back. Told him I washed my hands of him. Never wanted to hear from him again. He was a waste of space, Rory! A waste of space!'

He was growing too agitated. I stood up and put my arm round his shoulder.

'I'm sorry I asked you, Granda. It's just sometimes I wonder about him.'

I wanted to ask so much more, but it always ended the same way. My granda couldn't talk about it. It made him too angry.

Granda patted my hand. 'The only son I've got now is you, Rory. You're the best boy that ever lived. I don't need anybody else, and neither do you.'

But, at that moment, I thought perhaps I did. I was worried about my granda. I didn't like the way Mrs Foley was always asking questions about him, and I didn't like the way that people, really nice people, like Darren's mum, kept suggesting that Granda should be in a home.

4

My granda was nervous as we walked, or rather shuffled, up to the school on Parents' Night. We were late. That was because we had to go back when I realized that Granda was still in his slippers.

We were the last to arrive. All the other parents were waiting patiently in a queue, or flicking through jotters looking at schoolwork. I saw Mrs Foley glance up at us as we walked in, disapproval written all over her face. 'Lighten up!' I threw the thought at her.

Suddenly, Darren rushed over. 'Hello, Granda.'

I was kind of proud that my granda was everybody's Granda. Of course, Darren's grandfather was dead young looking; always tanned from holidays in Spain. Whereas mine, with his sparse grey hair and his wrinkles, couldn't be anything else but a granda.

'Hello, Darren, son.' Granda chucked him under the chin. 'How are you? Top of the class as usual?'

'Me? I'm bottom of the class.' Darren said it proudly. 'Always have been.' He said it as if it was a real achievement.

Granda looked around. 'OK, where is this Holy Foley?'

I felt my hair stand on end. 'Don't call her that to her face, Granda!'

Darren was already giggling. 'Aw, go on, Granda. I dare you. That would be such a laugh.'

'Darren, don't tell him that. She'll slaughter me!'

My granda was agitated. 'Och, Rory, you're getting me excited. I'm going to need the toilet now. Where is it?'

I knew there was something I forgot before we came out. I took his hand and led him to the toilets in the corridor. 'You know how to find your way back, don't you? The classroom right at the end. Maybe I should just wait for you.'

That insulted him. 'Goodness' sake, Rory. I'm not a baby. I'm old enough to be your granda.' He winked at me. 'I can go to the toilet on my own. I'm no' that daft . . . yet . . .'

Nevertheless, I couldn't keep still as I waited for him to return. I was beginning to have nightmares. What if he forgot to pull up his zip? He'd done that once when we went into the town. Embarrassing or what! Or, suppose he simply forgot why he was here, came out of the toilet and just went back home? He'd done that once when we went to the cinema. I had sat waiting for him for half an hour before I went out to look for him and found he'd just gone. When I finally arrived home he had the cheek to tell me off for being late!

I let out a sigh of relief when he stepped unsteadily back into the classroom. He hung his coat on a hook along with Mrs Foley's and waved over at me. He looked a little less nervous, and rubbed his hands together. 'OK, lead on,' he said.

Just at that moment, the couple who had been with Mrs Foley moved off and the teacher raised her eyes to us and beckoned us closer. 'Hello, Rory, and this must be Mister McIntosh. It's so nice to meet you at last.'

Mrs Foley beamed. Granda shook her hand firmly. 'I've heard a lot about you, Mrs Foley.'

Good so far, I thought. I almost whistled with relief.

'What I really wanted to talk to you about was Rory's homework —' she began, but my granda interrupted.

'I make sure he does his homework.'

'Yes, perhaps you do. Unfortunately, I never see it.' She raised an eyebrow and paused dramatically. I always felt as if Mrs Foley thought she was in a play. She was always acting. 'Strange things happen to Rory's homework,' she continued.

Granda was leaning forward, peering at her. Leaning so close that for one awful moment I thought he was going to kiss her. What he did was worse than that. No. Not what he did. What he said.

'You *have* got a moustache. I thought Rory was kidding me.'

Why don't floors open up and swallow you when you need them to? Mrs Foley was lost for words, for once. But my granda was smiling and nodding his head as if he'd just given her a lovely compliment.

What would have happened next we will never know. One moment I was waiting for Mrs Foley to either burst with indignation, or land a punch on my granda's chin. The next, her nose began to twitch. 'What is that smell?' she said.

Granda looked round innocently. 'That's smoke. Something's on fire.'

There was a yell from the other side of the room. Something *was* on fire. Granda's coat! There it was, clouds of smoke billowing from his pocket.

His pipe. Of course, the one thing I had forgotten. When my granda gets nervous he always needs a puff of his pipe and he'd obviously sneaked a puff while he was in the toilet.

'That's my coat!' Granda said as if he was totally surprised. As if it hadn't been him who had left his pipe smouldering there.

Now Mrs Foley screamed. 'And that's mine!' Because the coat hanging beside Granda's, pale green with a little matching scarf, was now on fire too.

Right at that moment the smoke alarms went off, screeching like banshees. The caretaker appeared and began ushering everyone out.

'Into the playground. Please! Step lively!'

'This is exciting,' my granda said, taking Mrs Foley's arm. 'Do you think the Fire Brigade's coming?'

They better not, I prayed. That would be all Mrs Foley would need.

It was Darren's dad who saved the day. He came running in with a bucket of water and threw it over the coats. End of panic.

Not for Mrs Foley. She sank into a chair. 'That coat was dry-clean only,' she said.

Granda found the whole thing funny and exciting, the way a boy would. The way Darren and the rest of my classmates did. The way, maybe I should have done. But all I could see was Mrs Foley looking at my granda. A look that seemed to say, you haven't heard the last of this.

At that moment I didn't know what she minded most, the fire or the fact that Granda had mentioned her moustache.

5

'*H*e's my hero! Your granda tried to set the school on fire! What a guy!' Darren was delighted with it. In fact, so were all my friends. They recounted the tale over and over, exaggerating it so that the whole school was left a smouldering pile of ruins and Mrs Foley was a chargrilled ghost of a teacher.

I only had a sick feeling when I thought about that night. Questions had been asked when the fuss had all died down, and Granda had admitted with relish that, yes, it must have been his fault. He didn't see the look that passed between the caretaker and Mrs Foley and even some of the parents. I had wanted to scream at them, 'It was an accident. Anyone can have an accident!'

'What did your mum say about it?' I asked Darren. His mum always had something to say about everything, but I liked her, and I knew she liked me.

Right away I knew I shouldn't have asked. Darren's smile wavered. 'She just said that it would have been awful if that had happened in the middle of the night. It could have been really dangerous.'

I tried to sound cheerful. 'It would never happen, because I hide his pipe before I go to bed, so he can't smoke it even if he wanted to.' I mean, did they think

I was daft? 'You mind and tell her that, Darren.'

'It worries my mum, Rory. She says that at your age you should be playing football. You shouldn't have that kind of . . .' He searched around for the word his mother had used. He'd never find it. He wasn't bottom of the class for nothing. But I knew what it was. I had heard it too often.

'Responsibility,' I said, and Darren nodded.

But if it wasn't my responsibility, then whose was it?

That was the week we met Val Jessup. She came to our door one evening just as I was laying the table for tea. She was a social worker, assigned to our case.

'I didn't know we had a case,' I told her.

'You're a social worker?' Granda said. 'You don't look old enough to be out of school.'

She didn't – bright-eyed, with clear skin and no make-up and shiny fair hair tied up in a ponytail. She was full of enthusiasm about ways to help us. I had a feeling we were her first 'case'.

'Did Mrs Foley send you?' I asked her as she sat in the living room going through Granda's pension books. She wanted to make sure he was getting his full range of benefits she said.

'Mrs Foley?' Her puzzled expression seemed genuine. 'No, it was actually your doctor who got us on to your case.'

Dr Nicol, of course.

Granda came shuffling into the room then. 'I don't

know what that daft doctor thinks we need a social worker for. Is this because he lost his homework?' Val Jessup looked even more baffled. 'It'll never happen again,' my granda assured her.

After she had gone, I began to think that having our own social worker wouldn't be such a bad thing. Val Jessup was going to organize a home help who would come in at lunchtime and make Granda something to eat. She would also make sure he took his medicine. Maybe, I began to think dreamily, I would be able to join the football team again.

Just before he went off to bed, my granda came in to my bedroom. 'She seems a nice girl, that Val Jessup. Reminds me of Grace Kelly.'

'Grace Kelly? Was that one of your old girlfriends, Granda?'

He sat on the bed. 'I wish. No, she was a film star. A beautiful film star who turned into a princess. She was one of my favourites.'

I didn't point out that they were all 'one of his favourites'.

'A beautiful film star who turns into a princess? Sounds like a fairy story, Granda.'

'It's as true as I'm sitting here.'

There was no point arguing with him. 'And does Val Jessup look like her?'

'Not at all.'

'So, how does she remind you of her, then?'

'Well,' he explained as if he was talking to an idiot, 'they've both got fair hair.'

Is it any wonder he's driving me potty? That didn't make any sense at all.

He began tucking me into bed, so tightly I couldn't move. 'There ye are, Rory, my boy, with that girl's help you and me are going to be just fine. And I'm going to try harder to look after you too.'

'You look after me just fine, Granda,' I said, meaning every word, remembering nights when my granda had made toffee apples for me, and put up Christmas trees, and carried me shoulder high at football matches. My granda looked pleased when I said that and he stood up and grinned toothlessly. His teeth even now would be smiling up from a glass in the bathroom.

'I feel that much better now,' he said with a big sigh.

'Now that we've got a social worker, Granda?'

He didn't even turn round to answer me. 'Not at all. No, now that my bowels have moved. That was three days and I hadn't been to the toilet.'

I groaned and pulled the duvet over my head. 'TOO MUCH INFORMATION!' I yelled, and I could hear the old devil chuckling all the way back to his bedroom.

A few days later, Mrs Foley was at it again. 'How are things at home now, Rory?'

'We've got a social worker,' I told her, hoping that would shut her up.

It didn't, but she seemed relieved. 'I'm glad about that at least. You do need some help.'

I decided to relieve her even more. 'We're getting a home help as well.'

She smiled at me. She actually smiled, and the sun caught her moustache and it sparkled. 'Oh wonderful.'

'You've made her day,' Darren said as the lunchtime bell rang. 'She's not so bad really.'

'Are you daft, Darren? Mrs Foley is evil beyond belief. You start thinking she's nice and she's got you under her evil spell.'

We raced out of the school gates together. Darren headed home and I ran for the bakery and two hot pies.

The baker was standing by his door as I came up. He took one look at me and shook his head. 'Oh, Rory, son. There's something going on at your flats. The Fire Brigade's been there and somebody got taken away in an ambulance.'

I felt the colour drain from my face and my blood really did run cold. Everything else was forgotten. I ran as if the devil himself were after me. A crowd had gathered round the building, and there were policemen guarding the entrance. I dodged through them but one of them grabbed me and held me back.

'Watch it, laddie. Where do you think you're going?'

I struggled with him. 'I live here. Where's my granda?'

It was then I spotted our neighbour, Mrs MacKay. She saw me too and she looked angry. 'I knew this would happen. I just knew that daft old idiot would set something on fire one of these days.'

I couldn't take that. I threw myself at her, lashed out with my foot to kick her. It was only the policemen holding me back that saved her.

'Don't you dare say that about my granda!'

I could see the policeman glare at Mrs MacKay and he knelt down to talk to me. He held me by the shoulders and he spoke to me softly. 'Your granda's gone to the hospital, but he's going to be all right.' He repeated that because I could feel a panic grow inside me and it showed. 'He's going to be all right. We'll get a car to take you to the hospital.'

'What happened? Why is he getting the blame? It might not have been his fault. I hid his pipe. I always hide his pipe when I'm not there.'

The policeman looked baffled at that. But I didn't want it to be my granda's fault. It could only lead to more trouble for us.

'I'm afraid it looks as if he left the chip pan on and forgot about it. Major cause of fires, son.'

A chip pan? What was my granda doing with a chip pan?

6

*I*t was a policewoman who took me to the hospital. I felt a knot in my stomach as she led me up the corridor to the room where my granda was. I kept hoping he would be sitting up in bed, winking at the nurses, hollering for cups of tea. But what if he wasn't?

What if, instead, he was . . .

No! I couldn't bear even the thought of that.

My granda would be fine. My granda was always fine. Nothing was going to kill my granda.

The policewoman talked all the way there, but I didn't hear a word she said. I tried to listen, but nothing registered. It was as if I were in a dream world as I walked through the hospital, with its white-panelled walls and nurses who moved smartly past me, and cleaners pushing trolleys. But it was a silent world, as if someone had turned the sound down.

Finally, we came to his room. A male nurse was at the door. I had a feeling he'd been waiting for me. 'Looking for Mister McIntosh?' He was smiling, but that didn't make me feel any better. It was a tight smile, a 'you have to be a brave boy' kind of smile.

'How's my granda?'

'He's suffered from smoke inhalation. He's very weak at the moment. We have him on oxygen . . .'

There was a lingering pause. 'He doesn't look too good.'

Was he trying to tell me my granda wouldn't make it? I felt the colour drain from my face. The nurse hurried on to reassure me. 'He's going to be OK. You've not to worry about that. But he'll need a lot of looking after.'

'I'll look after him,' I said quickly. And it was impossible to miss the glance that passed between the nurse and the policewoman. A warning bell rang somewhere deep inside me; too deep to bother me at that moment. All I wanted was to see my granda. 'Where is he?'

The nurse pushed open the door of the room and there he was. My knees buckled under me when I saw him. He had drips and needles attached and monitors bleeping all round him, and his face was covered with an oxygen mask. He looked like an alien out of *Star Trek*.

The policewoman gripped me. 'Are you OK, Rory?'

Of course, I wasn't OK. My granda looked dead. He looked just like a corpse. His waxen skin was stretched over his face and he didn't have his teeth in.

'Are you sure he's going to be all right?' I asked again.

He's not going to die? That's what I really wanted to ask, but I was too afraid of the answer.

'He looks worse than he is, but try not to worry about him too much. He's made of strong stuff, your grandfather.' The nurse pulled a chair across to the bed. 'Do you want to sit with him for a while?'

I was reassured by the warmth of my granda's hand when I touched it, and the steady rise and fall of his chest.

'You haven't had any lunch,' the policewoman reminded me. 'Can I get you anything?'

I couldn't have eaten a thing. All I wanted to do was to sit there, with my granda, and wait for him to open his eyes. The policewoman and the nurse left me alone, although now and then I would catch them peeking at me through the glass in the door.

I held tight on to my granda's hand and didn't care, for once, who saw it. I don't know how long I sat there. Dusk had fallen early on this wet, grey October day.

Please God let him wake up soon. I didn't pray very often. But I did now. I closed my eyes and sent up a special prayer.

'Listen, Big Man, my name's Rory. I know I don't talk to You much, but You're busy with wars and famine and things. And me and my granda are usually doing OK. So I hope You're going to listen to me now. I don't give You any trouble. So a bit of help here would be much appreciated. I want him to wake up. I promise I'll never shout at him again, even when he slurps his tea. I'll even listen to his endless stories about his bowel movements. I'll never moan or complain about him again . . . I promise . . . if You just let him wake up.'

*

Val Jessup came in later. She had a big smile on her face. A reassuring smile. 'I believe he's going to be all right,' she said brightly.

'I don't understand how it happened,' I told her. 'What was he doing with the chip pan. I always bring in pies.'

She pulled a chair up beside me and sat down. 'I suppose we'll have to wait until he wakes up before we know that.'

She'd brought me some sandwiches from the hospital canteen and she stayed with me while I ate them.

'Do you get paid overtime for this?' I asked her.

'Well, you are my client. My responsibility.' She was blinking and I suddenly thought she looked nervous, and there was that warning bell ringing again. Only louder this time.

'But it is getting late. We have to think of getting you to bed.'

'I'm staying here with my granda,' I said firmly.

'That's not possible, Rory. You need a good night's sleep. And probably by the time you come tomorrow he'll be sitting up and talking and feeling a lot better for knowing that you're being taken care of too.'

I could understand that. 'OK. I'll go home. Is the flat OK?'

Val Jessup looked even more nervous. 'No. But even if the flat were in a liveable condition, you know we couldn't allow you to stay there by yourself.'

My mind was beginning to panic, to sift through the other options open to me. I wanted to say I could stay at Darren's. But that was impossible. Darren had two little sisters, and his big brother and his girlfriend and their baby were all staying there too.

No room for one more.

'So where am I going?'

I didn't want to hear her answer. I knew what it was going to be.

'You're staying at the children's home at Castle Street.' As Granda's nightmare was Rachnadar, mine was the children's home at Castle Street. My face must have changed immediately. 'Now, don't look like that, Rory. It's only for a few nights till we work things out.'

My voice was trembling. I couldn't control it. 'I don't want to go there.'

'I know you don't, Rory, but we're going to look after you while your grandfather's in hospital. And it's not as bad as you think. The staff there are really nice people.'

I stared at my granda, willing him to open his eyes, leap out of bed and say, 'Let's go home, Rory, son.'

But he didn't. He didn't stir a muscle. And I didn't have the courage to scream and shout and refuse to leave him.

Thanks very much, Big Man, I thought. So much for an answer to my prayers. But I took it back right away. Because maybe this was His plan. Granda *would* feel better knowing I was being taken care of and, if I just put up with this, he would be fine tomorrow. Fighting fit.

So, I allowed myself to be led out of the hospital and into Val Jessup's car, and driven across town to the children's home at Castle Street.

The stuff of nightmares.

7

Castle Street seemed to loom at me out of the darkness – an old Victorian villa that had been converted into a children's home just after the war. Grey, dead stone, crow-step gables and even a turret – it looked just the kind of place wizards and warlocks would live in. It was silhouetted against the night sky as patches of cloud scurried across the moon and an eerie silver light was cast against the building.

Like something out of a ghost story.

I pushed that thought right out of my mind. I would not be afraid!

If I could just stop my heart from thumping.

Val Jessup drew her car to a halt and turned to me. 'You're going to be all right about this?'

As if I could say, 'NO!' I wanted to. I wished it could be last night and I could have hidden that stupid chip pan, thrown it down the chute with the rest of the rubbish. If I had, I would be home now with my granda, listening to him sucking his teeth, listening to his hearing aid whistling, annoying me as I tried to watch *Sportscene*. But it *had* happened. I was here. Nothing to be done about it.

'I'm only here till my granda's out of hospital. One night!' I snapped, and jumped out of the car.

The front door was hauled open even before we reached it. They'd been watching for us. A tall gangly youth stood there grinning, with a mug in his hand. 'Hello, you must be Rory?' He welcomed me like a long-lost brother. 'I'm Tony. Come on in and meet everybody.'

He led us into the kitchen where a group of boys and girls were sitting round the table, obviously having supper. A big platter of toast and cheese was in the middle and they were all getting stuck into it. I realized for the first time how hungry I was.

'This is the mad bunch,' Tony said amiably and immediately put me off him. What was he trying to do? Make them sound like an alternative lifestyle I might prefer? Forget it, pal.

He introduced the 'mad bunch' one by one. They didn't seem very mad to me. Jackie was black and he waved a hand at me. Georgie was a shy-looking blonde girl who smiled her greeting. Tom had ginger hair and pale skin. He stood up. 'Want some toast, Rory?' Without waiting for my answer he popped two slices in the toaster. 'There's cheese as well.'

Jackie patted the seat beside him. 'Take a pew. How's your grandpa?'

I glanced at Val. 'I told them your granda's not well, Rory. In hospital.'

I shrugged an answer. 'He's OK, I suppose.'

Val only stayed long enough to see me settled with a mug of tea and cheese on toast. Then she put my school bag beside me and began to leave. 'I'll be back in the morning,' she said, 'to take you to the hospital.'

As soon as she'd gone, Jackie and Tom started firing questions at me. 'You're not going to school tomorrow? Lucky old you!'

Tony was still grinning. 'Only for tomorrow. After that, it's business as usual.'

I don't think! If anyone thought I was going to school while my granda was lying unconscious . . . A sudden picture of him flashed into my mind, lying there, his breath only a rattle, his face like wax – and my appetite disappeared again.

'OK, Rory?' Tony touched my shoulder and I nodded.

He lifted my bag. 'I'll take this up to your room. You finish your supper.'

'I'm only here till my granda gets out of hospital,' I said when Tony had left the kitchen.

'Aye right! That's what they told me!' Jackie leaned across the table. ' "Just till your mother can cope again, son." That was three years ago.'

'Shut up, Jackie!' Georgie snapped at him. She didn't seem so shy any more. 'Remember how you felt the first night you came here. So how must Rory feel? And he's worried about his grandpa too.'

Suitably scolded, Jackie sat back. Georgie pushed the plate closer. 'Eat up,' she said.

'I call him my granda . . . not my grandpa.' Somehow it didn't sound like the same person, too posh. He was my granda, always would be.

'Sorry.' She smiled.

There was a sudden wild commotion from another room. A voice started shouting and swearing abuse. Everyone round the table stiffened. I froze. 'Who's that?'

'Tess,' Tom said. 'She goes berserk whenever they turn the television off and she has to go to bed. Says she was allowed to stay up all night if she wanted.'

'She shouldn't be here!' Jackie said angrily. 'I heard Tony talking today.' He touched his head. 'She's mad. Totally off the wall. You never know what she's going to do next.'

The really mad one, this Tess, flew into the kitchen like a tornado. A young woman was behind her, trying to hold her back, and she looked angry too. Tess turned on her.

'Don't you dare touch me. I'll tell my social worker you've been battering me!'

The woman shook her head at her. 'And of course she'll believe every word you say.'

Tess turned her piggy eyes on me. 'What's that!' Her voice was loud, almost a scream, as if she thought no one would hear her, or listen, unless she yelled.

I wanted to answer boldly. 'None of your business.' But my throat was suddenly tight and I couldn't say a word.

'This is Rory, Tess. He'll be staying with us for a while.'

That made my heart thump. For a while? For a while! NO!

'He's sitting in my seat!' Tess made a dive towards

me and I jumped out of the seat automatically. Self-preservation and all that. I was sure she was about to lift me out of the chair with one hand. She looked capable of it.

The young woman held her back. 'You're not sitting anywhere, Tess. You're going up to your room.'

In answer, Tess kicked at the table, sending mugs tumbling and tea spilling everywhere. We all jumped to avoid it.

'Ha!' Tess yelled in triumph. 'If I'm not sitting, nobody is.'

It took both the woman and Tony to drag her out of the kitchen while we were left to wipe the table with paper towels to mop up the tea.

'What is she so angry about?' I asked Jackie.

Jackie tutted. 'She's the type that'll always find something to be angry about.'

When Tony came back into the kitchen he tried to reassure me. 'She's not going to be here for long. They're arranging another place for her.'

'The local jail,' Tom put in and everyone giggled.

'Beside her ma,' Jackie laughed.

I didn't. 'I'll be out of here before she is,' I said. So I didn't care where she went, or when.

I was to sleep in a room with Tom and Jackie, in a bed snug in the corner, with fresh sheets and a soft white duvet. It looked inviting. If only it had been anywhere else but Castle Street.

I lay for such a long time trying to sleep, trying not to think, but my mind was a jumble of emotions.

What a day! This morning, just another ordinary day at school, and now my life had changed completely. I thought about my granda, and couldn't bear it. It hurt too much.

I could still hear Tess shouting in her room somewhere down the hall. I tried not to imagine her barging in here, dragging me out of bed, throwing me from the window. I'd heard the nightmare stories about what goes on in places like this. If I'd had the nerve I would have wedged a chair under the door handle.

I lay there, listening to Tess, clutching at the duvet, my knuckles white. I curled up like a baby and tried not to cry.

8

I did sleep eventually, but it was a strange, fitful sleep. 2 a.m. 3.10. 4.15. I followed the night hour by hour on the clock by my bed.

I was already dressed and ready by the time Tom and Jackie laughed their way into their school uniforms. They went to two different schools.

How could they seem so happy here? As if they hadn't a care in the world. I just wanted to go.

Tony popped his head round the door to tell us that breakfast was ready. He seemed surprised to see me sitting fully dressed on the bed.

'I was going to tell these two to keep quiet, not to wake you. We were going to give you a lie-in.'

'Val's coming for me,' I said.

'I know, but not till after nine.'

We went down to breakfast together, and the monster, Tess, was there too. She looked unkempt as if she'd slept in her clothes. The woman, who introduced herself as Nellie, sat close beside her, as if she was always ready to grab her before she reached out to wallop one of us.

I sat as far away from her as possible. Her pale eyes followed me and, though I never once made eye contact with her, I could feel her cold stare.

'How long's he gonna be here?' she demanded. 'Long enough for me to thump him, I hope.' Then she laughed as if she'd said something really hilarious.

'You'll not touch him, or anyone else,' Nellie said shortly. 'Now come on, your taxi's here.'

I waited until she was safely out of the house before I asked: 'She gets a taxi to school?'

Jackie answered in a posh voice. 'Tess gets a taxi everywhere, and it isn't school she goes to. She has a private tutor.'

'So, if you want special treatment, Rory, be as bad as you can be, and you'll get it.' Tom sounded bitter. Not a bit like how he normally sounded.

'Now, that's not true, Tom.' Tony tried to sound firm, and failed. It sounded more like it annoyed him too.

Tom carried on. 'Me and Jackie and Georgie, we've got to walk to school, rain or shine. But her? Oh no, we can't have poor little Tess getting her feet wet.'

Val arrived shortly after they left. Tony had phoned the hospital and, to my delight, they said my granda was awake and had even tried some breakfast.

The news burst out of me as soon as Val arrived.

'I know,' she said, beaming. 'I phoned the hospital too.'

*

I knew as soon as I stepped out of the lift that Granda was better. I could hear him, shouting at the top of his voice, thanking the nurses for all their hard work.

'You're wonderful people!' he was yelling. 'You deserve medals for all the work you do!'

'He always shouts like that. It's because he's deaf!' I explained to Val. 'I bet he's not got his hearing aid.'

I broke into a run and raced towards my granda's room.

He tried to struggle out of bed as soon as he saw me. 'Rory, my boy!' Just in time the nurse held him back and I leapt on to the bed beside him.

'Granda, I thought you were going to die.' Putting it into words brought the tears to my eyes, and I was glad no one could see me as my granda hugged me close to him.

'It would take more than a load of old smoke to kill me.'

I slipped off the bed and sat on a chair, but I still held tight on to his hand. 'What happened, Granda?'

'I was only trying to help. You were bringing in the pies, so I thought I'd make us some chips to go with them.'

I squeezed his hand. That really choked me up.

'You daft old devil!' I said. 'You left the chip pan on, didn't you?'

'I was looking for the potatoes. I was rummaging

in the wardrobe for them, and . . . that's the last thing I remember.'

He started to cough then because he was talking so much and he didn't stop until the nurse had brought him some water. He slurped it into his mouth.

'How do you feel, Granda?'

'Me? Fighting fit.' He then began to cough again, and I glanced at the nurse who stood beside him rubbing his back gently.

'Doctor will be in later to examine him.' She answered my unspoken question before she left us alone. Val went with her.

'Where did you sleep last night?' Granda asked. 'Did Mrs MacKay take you in?'

'That old bat? You've got to be joking.'

Her that had called my granda 'a daft old idiot'? There was no way I would have stayed with her, even if she had asked.

It was then I realized that my granda didn't know where I'd slept, and I didn't know how to tell him. 'I was fine,' I said.

'But where?' He nodded out to Val Jessup. 'Did that nice lassie let you stay with her?'

I wondered whether I should tell him a lie and say, 'Yes, Val Jessup had let me sleep in her spare room; we had sat up all night watching the television, ate chocolate ice cream and popcorn . . .'

My hesitation, however, was enough to put my granda on the alert. The truth began to dawn on him. 'You didn't get taken to that Castle Street?' His eyes

41

began to fill up. He was growing agitated. He knew, had always known, that Castle Street was my nightmare, just as Rachnadar was his.

'It was all right, Granda, honest. Everybody was dead nice.' I pushed from my mind a picture of terrifying Tess.

'No grandson of mine is going to Castle Street. Not while I'm alive.' He began shouting, struggling again to get out of bed. 'Nurse! Get my clothes. I'm getting out of here.'

He was already swinging his legs out of the bed. Coughing again. He was beginning to frighten me he was so agitated.

'I'm no bed-blocker!' He shouted. 'Get me out of here.'

The nurse came rushing in along with Val. Together they all managed to calm my granda down, but only after I assured him over and over that I would be settled in Castle Street until he was well enough to come home from hospital.

'Just you get better soon, Granda,' I kept telling him.

'I'll be out of here tomorrow, you wait and see!' he kept saying. 'And then you'll never have to worry about me again!'

I didn't want my granda to worry about me either. So, I determined there and then that I would go back to Castle Street. I had no choice. Though the thought of it terrified me even more now.

And not just because of the awful Tess.

I had seen the look that had passed between the nurse and Val when Granda had said, 'I'll be out of here tomorrow.'

I didn't know then what that look meant, but it scared me more than Castle Street.

9

When we left the hospital to let Granda rest, Val took me back to our flat. I looked around at the blackened walls, the smoke-damaged furniture and curtains. The air in the house was thick with the smell of smoke too.

I felt a lump in my throat when I saw my granda's mug lying on the coffee table in the living room. The daft old soul had probably made himself a cup while he waited for the oil in the chip pan to heat up. The paper lay on the floor. Had he been reading? Had he drifted off to sleep? Or had he really been on his knees in the bedroom looking for potatoes? We would never know.

I was caught between pure love for him, trying to help with the lunch, and exasperation with him. Because of this he had landed himself in hospital, and landed me in Castle Street.

Val tried to make me feel better. 'Come on, let's get your clothes.'

My clothes, even tucked away in drawers, or hung in the closet, smelt of smoke. I sniffed them and made a face at Val.

She began shoving things into a rucksack. 'We'll

get them into the washing machine as soon as we get to the . . .' She stopped. She'd almost said 'the home' but she changed it suddenly, 'to Castle Street.'

'I've put all my granda's pills in,' I told her as she took a bottle out of the rucksack. 'I better take them to the hospital.'

She shook her head. 'They don't allow any medicines in hospital. They supply their own.'

I shrugged and slipped the bottle back in my rucksack. I wasn't leaving any of his medicines here. If any of the gangs round here found out there was an empty flat with the chance of drugs, any kind of drugs, in it, they'd be breaking down the door before you could say 'temazipam'.

Before we left I took another look around the flat. 'Do you think I could get it painted before my granda gets out of hospital?' I was imagining a bright, white flat and the welcome that would be for him. 'I've got money in the building society. Not very much, but it would buy paint.'

Val waited until she was closing the door behind her before she answered that one. 'We don't have to think about that for the moment.'

What she said hung round me like a wet coat. Why didn't I have to think about that for the moment? How long would my granda be in the hospital? And how long was I going to have to stay at Castle Street, because I couldn't bear to stay there for long. And it was all because of this Tess. I had never come across anyone like her before. Her anger, her violence, scared

45

me. Scared us all. But, for some reason, it was me she had it in for.

Every day I was at Castle Street Tess seemed to grow angrier and always with me. One night, after we'd had tea, she suddenly leapt from her chair and went for me. All I'd said was that she must take after her mother from all I'd heard.

'I'll kill you for that, you weasel.' Then she called me a few things worse than a weasel and tried to strangle me. It took both Tony and Nellie to drag her off me. She was like a wild animal as they hauled her out of the kitchen. Her eyes were staring at me. 'I'll get you, you wait and see if I don't.'

Tony sat me down in the kitchen while everyone else was moved into the living room. 'Why is she like that, Tony? She's horrible. She's always so angry.'

'Because nobody wants her, Rory. That's the simple answer. That's the reason she's here. Her mother's in prison, and nobody else will take her. Her aunts don't want her and no foster parent will put up with her.'

'No wonder,' I snapped. 'She's a horror.'

Tony sighed. 'I know. She's her own worst enemy. But you shouldn't be frightened of her. She's sad. You should feel sorry for her.'

Tess was still screaming somewhere upstairs. I decided that I wouldn't bother feeling sorry for her. I'd just go on being frightened of her.

But I had to get out of here!

I wanted home.

My granda felt the same. Every day after school, Val Jessup would pick me up at Castle Street and drive me to the hospital to visit him and he would ask the same question: 'Is everything OK in that place?'

And I would tell him the same lie: 'Hunky-dory, Granda.'

Then my granda, not believing a word of it, would start shouting at the nurses. 'Get me out of here! Who's hiding my clothes?'

Yet, when was he getting out of there? To me, he seemed fine now. No more wheezy breathing. Better every day. One day he even told me that John Wayne had been in to visit him. 'He was in Army uniform. Fine figure of a man,' he told me.

'John Wayne, the film star? I thought he was dead.'

'He was standing where you are, Rory. Ready to go out and fight a war and save the world. But he popped in to see how I was doing first.' Granda called over one of the nurses at the next bed. 'Is that not right, nurse?'

She laughed. 'You were watching a John Wayne film on television, Mister McIntosh.'

That bothered me. I didn't want them thinking my granda was daft.

'He'd just fallen asleep. It could happen to anybody,' I said to her. She didn't look as if she believed me.

'Don't say things like that, Granda,' I told him as she moved off. 'Next time a film star comes to visit you, don't tell anybody but me.'

He was tutting away in annoyance. 'You're as bad

as that woman I had in this morning. Wanted to know if I knew the name of the prime minister. She needed me to tell her that? Is she daft? Who am I supposed to be, Mastermind?'

Someone had come in to question him, ask him daft questions? Why?

That night, Val phoned to say that tomorrow she would pick me up after school as usual. Before I visited Granda she had something important to talk to me about. She wouldn't tell me on the phone what that something was.

But the thought of it sent a chill through me that lasted all that night.

10

*N*ext morning, Mrs Foley was exceptionally nice to me. To be fair she had been ever since my granda had been taken into hospital, asking me every morning how I was, always insisting that I tell her anything that might be bothering me about life in Castle Street. She had also organized flowers to be sent to my granda from my class, and a big card with everyone's name on it.

That morning she held me back as we crowded out of her classroom. The first thing she asked was how things were at Castle Street.

My hesitation was all she needed to tell her something was wrong. Her eyes went wide with alarm and her moustache quivered. 'Has anything happened? Has anybody hurt you? I told you before, you can tell me.'

She seemed *so* concerned, I did exactly that. I told her about Tess. For once I wasn't embarrassed because I was scared of that monster of a girl. Tess wasn't a girl. She wasn't even an animal. She was more like some strange alien creature that no one could communicate with – and whose mission was to destroy life on earth!

Mrs Foley listened intently. When I'd finished she

stood up straight. 'You should not be in that place, Rory,' she said very firmly, as if she'd come to a decision.

'It's only till my granda comes home. He'll be out of the hospital tomorrow . . . or the next day.' How I wished that when I said that someone would agree with me. But what Mrs Foley did was disturbing. She avoided looking at me. She just muttered, 'Yes, of course.'

She patted me gently on the shoulder as I left her classroom. 'I'm going to give Val Jessup a phone.' She said with a little whiskery smile.

I'd seen her and Val talking before, when Val took me to school, huddled together, discussing me. It annoyed me.

In the playground, Darren was waiting impatiently for me. 'What did Holy Foley want?'

When I told him, it was Darren who was alarmed.

'What's wrong?' I asked him. 'She was only being nice . . . for once.'

Darren wasn't so sure. 'My mother says . . .' Darren lowered his voice, pulled me closer by the collar so I could hear his whisper. 'My mother says that Mrs Foley is such a nice woman, she'll probably want to foster you.'

If Darren had hit me with a sledgehammer he could not have shocked me more. I was gasping for breath. 'No way! No way!'

Darren nodded. 'Yes way. Think about it, Rory.' He started counting our teacher's good deeds on his fingers. 'She's really worried about you being in Castle Street. She's always having secret conversations with Val Jessup. She's a Christian. I rest my case.' He finished solemnly.

Fostered by Mrs Foley? The idea brought me out in a cold sweat. Why had I told her about Tess?

Yet, why was I so worried? 'My granda gets out of hospital tomorrow . . . or the next day,' I assured Darren, and myself. 'So it's hardly worth her while.'

Darren put all my fears, silent until now, into words. 'Are you sure about that, Rory? Maybe your granda's not doing as well as you think he is.'

I tried, for the rest of that morning, to put all these terrors from my mind. It didn't work. I felt as if a lump of concrete lay in my stomach. By lunchtime I couldn't take it any more. I had to reassure myself my granda was OK. I needed to talk to him.

I mumbled to Darren that I was going home. I felt sick. Home, I thought bitterly. I didn't have a home any longer. I would never have again if my granda didn't get better. NO! That wouldn't happen. Granda would be coming home tomorrow . . . or the next day.

When I left school I ran, not to Castle Street, but straight for the hospital.

I stepped quietly past the six-bedded wards and headed for my granda's room. Patients were either dozing on top of beds or sat silently reading. No one even looked up as I passed.

There were no nurses at the station outside

Granda's room so I was able to tiptoe closer to the door and push it open.

'Granda ... it's only me,' I began, but I didn't finish. My lips went dry. I'm sure my heart stopped.

My granda had gone. The bed had been stripped. Even his teeth and his hearing aid had disappeared from the top of his empty locker. Empty. Gone.

My first horrible thought was ... my granda was dead.

11

*N*ow everything that had happened seemed to fall into place. The strange looks that passed between the nurses whenever Granda would assure me he was getting better, as if they knew something I didn't. Granda hadn't been getting better. Granda had been dying.

Val Jessup needed to speak to me today. She'd been planning to meet me at Castle Street to tell me the truth.

My granda was dead.

They had let him die and I hadn't even been with him. I'd kill someone for this.

'Granda!' I yelled as loud as I could. 'Granda! Where are you?'

I wanted it to be a game. I wanted my granda to jump out at me, toothless and laughing at his joke.

Suddenly, the staff nurse came flying into the room. 'What are you doing here, Rory?'

'Where's my granda? He's dead, isn't he?'

I tried to push past her, but she held me firm. 'Listen to me, Rory.'

But once I started I couldn't stop. 'My granda's dead. You've let him die!'

Two other nurses rushed into the room to help her

calm me. She ordered one of them out of the room abruptly. 'One of you phone Val Jessup. The number's on my desk. The other, come and help me with Rory.'

She was finding it hard to hold me as I struggled to be free of her grip.

She held me by the shoulders. 'Rory, please listen to me.' Her voice was calm, trying to calm me too. 'Rory, your Granda is not dead.'

Those words were all I needed to hear. I stopped struggling and looked deep into her eyes. 'Are you telling me the truth?'

She nodded and smiled and led me to a chair by the window. 'He's fine. We had to move him, that's all.'

'Move him?' I repeated. 'To another ward? Which one? Can I go and see him now?' I was on my feet again.

'Val will take you to see him.' She said it very slowly. 'She'll be here soon.' She smiled at the nurse by her side. 'Nurse Long, go and fetch Rory some orange juice and a sandwich. How about that, Rory?'

I had to be sure. 'My granda's definitely not dead?'

Now the staff nurse laughed. She was a really pretty lady. Staff Nurse Maureen, she had told us. My granda had confided in me, only the other night, that he really fancied her. 'That beautiful red hair. She reminds me of Rhonda Fleming.'

'Another old girlfriend?' I had asked.

I might have known. Not an old girlfriend, but some old film star.

He had whispered. 'See, if I was just ten years younger . . .'

'Ten years, Granda? In your dreams,' I had told him. 'Make that thirty years, or even forty.'

The age difference didn't bother Granda. 'You wouldn't say that to Sean Connery.'

'Sean Connery hasn't got a hearing aid, nor keeps his false teeth in a glass by his bed. And I bet he's not always talking about his bowels.'

The memory of that conversation made me smile. My smile reassured Staff Nurse Maureen. 'Right. Why don't you come into my office and wait for Val.'

I was just finishing up a hot sausage roll when Val arrived. As soon as she came in, Staff Nurse Maureen stood up to leave. 'I'll leave this to you, shall I?' she said, and the look that passed between them made me feel as if I was about to throw up the sausage roll. They were still keeping something from me.

I was on my feet as soon as the staff nurse closed the door behind her. 'Right, where's my granda? Something's wrong. I know it.'

Val Jessup sat down and pulled me into the seat across from her. She had really unusual grey eyes, like smoked silver, and now they looked troubled. 'We've had to move your granda, Rory. It's been a difficult decision for everyone.'

'What do you mean . . . a difficult decision? Move him where?'

'You're just a boy, Rory. You can't take the responsibility of your grandfather, not any more.'

'What is it you're saying?' Why couldn't they just tell me the truth?

'I don't think your grandfather will be able to come home with you. He's been assessed, and it's been decided that he's just not fit enough.'

'You mean he has to stay in hospital for a while?'

OK, I thought, I can handle that . . . still trying to push the terrifying thought of Castle Street away.

But she didn't answer me. She hesitated just long enough for an awful truth to trickle through my thick mind.

'For always? Is that what you can't tell me? Is my granda never going to get home?'

She knelt down in front of me and squeezed my hand. 'You'll see him all the time, Rory. Honestly. It's for the best.'

My granda in hospital for always. What hospital? Not this hospital.

I began to shake. 'Where have you put him?' I was shouting again. 'Where is my granda?'

But I knew the answer to that before she told me. 'Rachnadar.'

12

I had never seen my granda cry – not even when my gran died. Then, his chin had trembled, but he'd been so strong, strong for me. It was me who couldn't handle losing my gran. That had almost broken my heart. I had learned what that phrase meant then; a broken heart. I felt as if my heart had been smashed like concrete, into tiny little bits. My granda had mended it. I still had my granda I kept reminding myself. We still had each other.

So, when I stepped into the ward at Rachnadar and found my granda sitting on a bed, with tears streaming down his face, I couldn't handle it at all. I burst into tears too and ran to him. Val Jessup stood back, her eyes filled up.

My granda hugged me and sobbed. 'Rory, son, what am I doing here? I thought they were taking me home, to surprise you, and they took me here.'

Then he stood up unsteadily. 'Are you here to take me home now?' His eyes brightened.

That only made me cry more. 'I can't, Granda. They won't let me.'

'But there's nothing wrong with me.' My granda gripped my shoulders, pleading with me. 'Don't let me stay here. This is where they put old folk that nobody wants.'

I glanced into the corridor, watched the shuffling old people with dead eyes pass up and down, going nowhere.

'I want you, Granda. You know I want you.'

My granda held my hand so tight it hurt. 'I've let you down, son. I've let your gran down. I promised her I'd look after you, and where have you ended up? In Castle Street of all places. Oh, your gran'll be cursing me upside down.'

He was growing more and more agitated. I sat beside him and put my arm round his shoulders. 'Granda, you've never let me down. I'll tell my gran that when I say my prayers. Don't you talk like that, Granda.'

But nothing I said would quieten him. The nurses had to come in and give him something to make him sleep and that was the worst thing of all. He lay back on his pillows and just stared at me, till eventually they flickered and closed.

To add to this awful day, when I got back to Castle Street, Terrible Tess was at her worst, yelling about how much she hated everybody. Nellie took her in to the TV room while everyone had tea, but she couldn't hold her. Tess was in a bad mood and she wanted to make sure she ruined everybody else's day. Finally, I couldn't take it any more. I'd had a worse day than anyone, and I was ready to shout at someone. It might as well be her.

'Belt up!' I leapt to my feet. 'Everybody here's fed up listening to you. We've all got problems, so shut your gob.'

I took everyone by surprise, especially Tess. But only for a second. Her eyes went wild and before I could jump out of the way she had thrown herself across the table at me. Dishes skidded everywhere. She grabbed hold of my shirt so tightly it was choking me, and the force of her sent us both reeling on to the floor. I tried to get to my feet, but Tess was strong and vicious. But I was angry too, and this time I wasn't so frightened of her. I had never been in a fight in my life. I hadn't expected my first one to be with a girl . . . well, almost a girl . . . and I held myself back from punching her.

Tess had no qualms about punching me. She landed one right against my nose, so hard I bit my tongue and I tasted sweet blood.

Nellie and Tony were on us in a flash, pulling her off me, while she cursed me with every swear word I had ever heard and some I'm sure she made up.

'I'll make you so sorry you said that, Rory McIntosh. You just wait and see.'

This is the worst day of my life, I thought, as I lay in bed, with Tess's threats still ringing in my head.

But the days grew worse.

At school, the idea of Mrs Foley actually fostering me loomed over me, like a bird of prey. At Castle Street, Tess had to be watched constantly as I waited

59

for her at any moment to launch herself at me again. And at Rachnadar, my granda retreated further and further into a shell.

One day, I found him at the emergency exit beside his room, staring out across the grounds. 'Are you OK, Granda?' I asked him. Stupid question. Of course he wasn't.

He didn't even look at me. 'This would never have happened in my young day. People then cared about each other. Looked out for each other. Now . . . nobody cares about anybody but themselves. It's a horrible world, Rory.'

I had never heard my granda talk like that and it scared me.

'If I were younger,' he went on, 'I'd run away from here. To somewhere they'd never find me.' And he rattled the iron bar on the door so loudly a nurse came running over to him and led him back to his bed.

'Now, now, Mister McIntosh, behave yourself. You're not helping your grandson with this behaviour. You naughty boy.'

She was talking to him as if he were a little baby. My granda! I was so angry I shouted at her. 'He can behave any way he wants. He's the best granda in the world.'

She simpered at me and left, and my granda said nothing. He just sat on the bed and stared at the floor.

'My granda's dying in there,' I said to Val as she drove me back to Castle Street.

She tried her best to cheer me up. 'Once he's settled you wait and see the difference. He'll be fine.'

I knew that wasn't true. He might breathe and walk and eat but, inside, my granda would be dead.

When we went into Castle Street, Tony was in the kitchen bathing his face. His cheek was scratched and bleeding. 'Tess,' he told Val. 'I've told them they have to find another place for her right away. She simply can't stay here.'

But she was here now, and for how long would they be able to watch her before I was the one with the bleeding face? Maybe I'd be fostered first by Mrs Foley. I didn't know what was the better option.

I lay in bed that night and tried to sleep. But all I could see every time I closed my eyes was my granda, standing at the emergency exit, gazing out with glassy eyes and saying, 'If I were younger I'd run away from here to somewhere they'd never find me.'

Suddenly, I shot up in bed. Wide awake.

Suddenly, I knew what I had to do.

Me and my granda were going to run away.

13

*I*t was a pitch-black night. Not even a moon to light my way, but I was glad of that. I'd never done anything like this before, never felt so nervous in my life. Never planned anything with such precision.

The Great Escape.

It had been three days since I'd decided. Three days, putting together my plan, organizing everything I had to do.

First, where would me and my granda go when we did escape? It was Darren, good old Darren, who'd come up with the solution to that one. Darren was the only person I'd confided in. 'Go to my mum's caravan,' he had said. (Darren's dad never seemed to own anything according to Darren. Everything was his 'mum's'.) 'She's closed it up for the winter. It's dead secluded. Nobody would ever find you there.'

Darren thought my plan was the most daring and exciting thing he'd ever heard of. He was desperate to help. Desperate to join me. I had sworn him to secrecy.

'You've got to promise me you won't say a word. On your cat's grave. Promise!' Darren was really attached to that cat of his.

So he had promised and I believed him. It was

settled between us, in whispered conversations in the playground, and Darren sneaked me the spare key of the caravan. All the time it seemed to me that Mrs Foley had been watching us suspiciously.

'I think you should go soon, Rory,' Darren said. 'Old Holy Foley's got plans for you.'

The sooner the better, I thought, as I saw my granda grow more quiet and confused each day.

Dying inside, I kept telling myself. But not for long. Once I had him out of there, he'd begin to live again.

Not that I could tell my granda my plans. He was so deaf I'd have to shout them out and half the hospital would hear. Mind you, the other inmates wouldn't hear me either. They were as deaf as my granda. But the nurses, the orderlies, the doctors, seemed to be always watching, always listening. I felt they were like warders in a prison, or jailors in a prisoner-of-war camp.

All I could do when I visited him was squeeze his hand and mouth to him, 'It's going to be all right, Granda, you wait and see.'

I went over and over in my head my plan, every step of the way. I had to be sure nothing could go wrong.

During visiting I would wedge open the door of the emergency exit. I'd seen this door wedged open like that often, and I was sure the nurses wouldn't check it till bedtime. Then, after Val dropped me at Castle Street, I would pick up our rucksacks – one for me, one for my granda – and sneak back and get into the

63

hospital that way. I would take my granda and we would creep out, through the wooded grounds, to the old back road and the station. There we could catch a late-night train down the coastal line to the park where Darren's mother had her caravan. I'd spent lots of days down there with Darren. Their caravan was set high on the hill overlooking the river, with a clear view of the coast road.

I had gathered up clothes for my granda, even his underwear, one day when Val had taken me back to the flat. Normally I wouldn't go near my granda's underwear, let alone touch it, but now I had no choice. (If Val thought I was too long in my granda's room she must have assumed I wanted to be alone. She couldn't have imagined my frantic efforts to cram as much as I could into a bag.) It seemed lucky too that I had taken all his pills with me that first day at the flat; almost as if I knew that one day I would need them.

That day at school, all I thought about was escape. I was shaking when Val took me to visit Granda that night.

'Maybe you're coming down with something,' she said, noticing my shivering. I just nodded.

She always left me alone with my granda while she had coffee with the nurses. That was my chance to wedge open the emergency exit.

If my luck held I wouldn't be missed for a few hours at least. And, by that time, hopefully, me and my granda would be long gone.

Later that night, everything went like a dream. There I was back at the emergency exit. The door eased open without a squeak.

I tiptoed inside. My granda was sitting on the bed, looking lost and alone. He was still fully dressed. I knew the nurses were always busy first with the bed-ridden patients, before getting the rest to bed. The curtains of the next cubicle were drawn round. As soon as my granda saw me, his eyes lit up. He got to his feet. 'Rory, my boy. Have you come back to visit me?' He started shambling towards me.

I put my finger to my lips. 'Shh, Granda. I've come to rescue you.' I glanced up the dimly lit corridor. No one was about. In the distance I could hear music from a radio and the nurses laughing and chatting. I pulled Granda back to his bed. 'We're going,' I tried to tell him, but he couldn't understand. Not yet.

I searched quickly for his coat and slipped it over his shoulders. My granda looked baffled, didn't know what was going on. All the time I was stuffing every-thing I could find into one of the rucksacks. His teeth were on the bedside table. Better not forget them. And his hearing aid, not that it did him any good; he usually forgot to switch it on.

'What are you doing, son?' he asked in a too loud voice.

My hands were shaking as I helped him into his coat. Every second I expected one of the nurses to come bustling into the room. Any second the whole escape plan would be in ruins. Now I knew how those prisoners felt in the old black-and-white war films my granda loved watching. Escaping from prisoner-of-war camps, wading through mud, with drooling guard dogs straining at their leashes and searchlights skimming the ground looking for them. Always the threat of being shot at dawn if they were caught.

Well, me and my granda wouldn't be shot at dawn. But would our fate be any better if we were caught? Separated forever, and my granda dying slowly. No. No matter what, we couldn't be caught.

'Come on, Granda. We're going.'

At that point, just as we were on the verge of leaving, I realized with horror that my granda was still wearing his slippers. Could I risk taking him in his slippers? No. Not worth double-pneumonia.

I pushed him back down on his bed. 'Come on, Granda, get your shoes on.'

'Where am I going, son?' he asked me again as I pushed his feet into his shoes. I looked up at him and a wave of love swept over me. My granda looked just like a little boy, as if he were my baby brother, relying on me to make things better, just as I'd always relied on my granda.

Well, I would make things better. I stood him up and took his hand. 'Come on, Granda.' My voice was barely a whisper, yet for once I knew he heard me. 'I'm getting you out of here.'

14

*I*t was as if God wanted us to escape, I kept thinking. He had listened to my prayers and decided
I was worth helping. Because, after we left the hospital by the emergency exit, everything went so
smoothly.

Not a soul saw us as we made our way, stealthily,
across the grounds of Rachnadar.

Ha! Stealthily! Bit of an exaggeration here. My
granda kept walking into bushes or stepping on nettles
and yelling. 'Och ya b-b-b . . .' And I would have to
shoosh him noisily. Once he even fell flat on his face
when he tripped on some bracken and he let out
another ear-piercing yell.

'Granda! You'd have been rubbish trying to sneak
out of a prisoner-of-war camp. We'd have been shot
by now,' I told him as I helped him to his feet.

'Eh? What? I can't hear you. I've not got my hearing aid in.'

Yet, in spite of all the noise my granda made, no
one was alerted. Even at the station just outside the
grounds no one saw us. The station was unmanned
and the platform was deserted. When the train did
roll in, it was almost empty. The ticket collector didn't
appear − too busy chatting up some blonde in a

faraway carriage. We sat alone the whole journey till we reached our final destination.

Final destination . . . ominous words.

However, if all that didn't mean that God was on our side, then I knew nothing about the Big Man.

My granda was like a little boy, allowing himself to be led, without a word, without a question. Safe in the knowledge that I would look after him.

The train's final stop was at the pierhead where passengers could connect with the ferries that sailed to the islands or the towns on the other side of the river. I had planned that if anyone did see us, then that's where they would look for us first. They would believe we had gone on to one of the islands, or to some town far down the Clyde. Even my granda thought that's where we were going.

'We're going on a boat, son?'

I shook my head. No point trying to explain, then. Granda couldn't hear a word I was saying. Instead, I took his hand and led him out of the deserted station. Only the porter was there, standing with his back to us – didn't even see us step off the train, and certainly didn't notice us leaving.

Outside, a fine drizzle had begun to fall. The kind of rain that seeped into your bones.

'Not far now, Granda,' I mouthed to him, trying to keep his spirits up for the journey ahead.

Because it was a journey, and all uphill, first along the coast road and then up the long, winding path that led to the caravan site. I could hear my granda's exhausted panting, but when ever I turned and asked him, 'Are you all right, Granda?', he would only grin and squeeze my shoulder and urge me on.

Please, God, I prayed silently. Please don't let him die before we get to this caravan. If You could just keep him going I promise I'll go out every Saturday collecting for the Salvation Army. I'll even join if that's what You want.

I stopped a few times to let my granda catch his breath. I could see the strain on his face, wet with the rain. I hoped I was doing the right thing. My granda could be in a warm, cosy bed right now. So could I.

But then, I reminded myself, I kept reminding myself, the bed would be in Rachnadar and my granda was dying from the inside there.

No. If my granda was going to die, at least he would die free.

Darren's mum's caravan was in a secluded spot, a good distance away from all the other caravans. 'A prime location', she had always boasted to me. 'I really don't like mixing with the type of people who own all the other caravans.'

My granda had laughed himself silly at that. 'They've probably moved their caravans far away to be rid of her. She's a right snob.'

Whatever the reason, I was glad now it was so secluded. Here, in the winter-deserted site, me and my granda could stay in comfort while I worked out what to do next.

It was worth everything when I saw my granda's

eyes go wide with delight as he realized where we were going. 'You're a genius, son,' he roared and he laughed so hard it carried through the misty rain, up through the trees, across the river.

The caravan was luxury. Only the best for Darren's mum. There were two bedrooms and a fitted kitchen. There was a bathroom with a shower. I opened the cupboards. Just as Darren had told me, they were crammed full of tins and packets. There was tea and coffee and sugar and cereals and dried milk.

'My mum's always scared we might get snowed in and have to fend for ourselves. It never occurs to her that we're only here in the summer.'

Thank goodness for your mum, Darren, I thought. I turned to my granda to show him the shelves stocked with food. 'Look, Granda, are you hungry?'

And to my surprise there he was standing, staring at me, tears streaming down his face.

I was suddenly afraid. He was old. He was sick. And now he was wet and exhausted.

My granda shook his head. 'I'm a lucky man, Rory. A lucky, lucky man.' He took a step closer to me and touched my cheek. 'What did I do to deserve a boy like you? You're the most special boy that ever lived.' He looked around the caravan. 'You've done all this for me?'

I knew I was ready to cry myself. I wanted to tell him that I had done this for both of us, so we could be together, the way we were meant to be. I couldn't bear the thought of my granda in Rachnadar, as much as I couldn't bear to be in Castle Street. I wanted to tell him that I would do anything so we could be together. Anything.

But the words wouldn't come. There was a lump in my throat that stopped me from speaking. So I made a joke of it.

'You know me, Granda. Boy with a heart of gold. So you better leave me all your money. Right?'

'Money! I've not got any money. But I've got a treasure map and hidden gold.' Then he chuckled. 'Or was that Humphrey Bogart?'

We had tea and biscuits and Granda settled himself in Darren's mum and dad's bedroom. He was shocked at the pink frilly curtains and duvet. 'Does her man sleep in here? What a wimp he must be.'

After he had gone to sleep I stood out on the veranda, looking over the river. The rain had cleared and the moon sparkled on the water. We would have been missed by now. Both of us. The alarm would have been raised in Castle Street and in Rachnadar. But only Darren knew where we were and he was my best friend. He would never tell. He had promised to text me if they did find out where we had gone.

No matter what, I knew I had done the right thing. We were never going back. I knew that night that I would die before I'd let them separate me and my granda again.

15

*T*he first thing I did when I woke up was to check my text messages. I had this awful feeling that Darren had texted me in the night, warning me, and I'd been sound asleep.

But there were no messages. No one had called.

The clock by my bed said eight o'clock. I would get up and make my granda his morning coffee. He loved his coffee. Then I'd give him his morning pills.

But when I walked into the kitchen I was startled to find my granda was already there, still in his pyjamas, making coffee for me!

At least, he thought it was coffee. He was actually spooning Bisto into a cup.

'Granda, what are you doing up?'

'I'm fighting fit! I'm A1. Sit you down and have your breakfast.' My granda had set the table too. Two mugs, a knife, marmalade and crackers.

'No milk,' he told me cheerily. 'But she's got some whitener stuff.'

I just hoped it wasn't arsenic!

He was amazing me. It was as if, this morning, I had my old granda back. Capable, in charge, looking after me. I felt so good, I began to sing – an old

Frank Sinatra number that I knew he loved. He was always singing Frank Sinatra songs.

My granda joined in, out of tune and singing all the wrong words. For me, it was the best breakfast I had ever eaten. There was no Tess haunting my dreams now, threatening me. And my granda was here with me.

After we'd eaten, we went out for a walk. We went along the hill path with the river view on one side and deep woods on the other.

'I could go a puff of my pipe.' He looked at me hopefully.

I shrugged. 'Sorry, Granda. I forgot it. Anyway, the doctor told you to give it up. It was bad for you.'

'You forgot my pipe! Are you daft or something?'

I thought that was a bit of a cheek. 'I had a lot to remember – your pills, your teeth, your hearing aid. There's that many bits of you to remember! You're never grateful.'

'But my pipe!' he kept saying. 'I can't believe you forgot that!'

The day, however, the scenery and most of all, freedom won him over in the end.

'This is lovely,' he said, sounding brighter than I'd heard him for such a long time. 'I used to come here when I was a boy. It wasn't a caravan site then. It was a Boy Scout camp. Used to fish in the pond in the woods.'

There was an overgrown path that still led to the pond. 'I caught many a good fish in that water.'

'Maybe you could fish again, Granda. Catch us something for our tea.'

The idea appealed to my granda. 'Aye, anything would be better than the junk she keeps in her cupboards.'

I thought that was a bit unfair, but I didn't say anything. After all, Darren's mum's 'junk' was going to keep us going for a while.

That was how we spent the afternoon – Granda used a stick and some string and an old bit of wire and sat on a rock at the edge of the pond dangling his rod into the water.

'Oh yes, you're going to catch Jaws with that thing,' I said to him.

'Ach, you shut up, boy. I'm a natural at this fishing.'

'You wish, old man. I better go and open a tin of salmon. That's the only fish we'll be eating tonight.'

But it didn't matter if he didn't catch anything, I thought. It's keeping him busy, making him feel useful.

Granda started singing at the top of his lungs.

'Granda, somebody'll hear you.'

We were supposed to be undercover. Some undercover, with my granda belting out Frank Sinatra at the top of his voice, and me having to shout at him to shut up.

He stopped suddenly and clamped a wrinkled hand over his mouth. 'Oops, sorry, son. Keep forgetting. I'm that happy, you see.'

Just at that moment, his line grew taut and began to jerk. 'Got one!' he yelled.

I raced towards him, grabbed the line to help him pull.

'Thar she blows!' my granda called, and I was too excited to tell him to keep quiet.

Together we hauled at the line and suddenly a struggling silver fish broke the surface. Granda swung it on to the bank, whooping like a cowboy who's just wrestled a steer.

'It's a biggun!' he said. 'How about a nice bit of trout for your tea?'

I looked closer. 'Is it a trout?'

My granda chuckled. 'I don't care if it's a piranha. We're eating it.'

We both fell on the bank beside the still-struggling fish, still gasping and fighting for its life. I almost felt like throwing it back. But hunger took over.

'Sorry, pal,' I said. 'But you can eat us if we ever fall in the water. Honest.'

We laughed so much my granda almost lost his teeth.

We laughed so much we almost didn't hear the bushes crackle behind us.

We laughed so much we almost didn't hear the footsteps.

16

I felt myself tense. Footsteps, so close, and no time to get away, to hide. We were going to be caught. Taken back to Castle Street, and Rachnadar. No. I wouldn't let that happen. I lifted a thick branch from the ground and shot to my feet. I stood defiantly between my granda and whoever it was coming through those bushes.

Just let anyone try to take us back!

All these thoughts swept through my mind like a bushfire. My granda still hadn't heard the footsteps, too engrossed in his fish.

It was only when two figures burst through the undergrowth that he even looked up.

Two people, a man and a boy. Father and son, if I judged correctly. They looked as wary of me as I was of them.

The man took a step in front of the boy. He had a weather-beaten face, and his clothes looked scruffy – a black jacket that had once belonged to a suit and pale, faded jeans. The boy seemed to be about the same age as me. His black hair was curly and his eyes bright blue in an unwashed face.

'What are you two doing here?' He asked it so

cheekily he got my back up. As if this place belonged to him.

'What's it to you?' I said just as cheekily.

The boy's father touched his shoulder to quieten his son. 'We've not seen you here before? Do you live here?'

I shook my head, not sure how to answer them, or even if I should. 'No,' I said finally. 'Just visiting.' I swallowed a lump in my throat, sure they could see I was lying. 'My granny's got a caravan.' I waved vaguely in the opposite direction to where Darren's mum's caravan was situated.

Suddenly, my granda took me by surprise. He had been watching the man warily and now he stood up unsteadily and spoke in a voice that was harsh and unfriendly. 'Here! You two get the hell away from us and mind your own business.' He didn't sound like my granda at all.

'Granda!'

The man's voice when he answered was just as harsh. 'Aye, you mind your business and I'll mind mine, old man.' He pulled at the boy's sleeve. 'Come on, Tyrone.'

Tyrone stared at me. His eyes were as unfriendly as the man's voice. He moved off behind his father and seconds later they disappeared into the undergrowth again.

'Granda! That was really rude.'

'Tinkers!' My granda spat the word out in disgust. 'Don't trust 'em. Don't like 'em.'

77

'I don't think you're supposed to call them tinkers any more, Granda. It's not politically correct. They're travellers.'

Granda tutted. 'Tinkers! They would be after my fish.'

'Travellers,' I insisted. 'And they wouldn't be interested in your old fish.'

Granda lifted his fish and started walking back to the caravan. 'Tinkers!' he kept muttering.

I was grinning as I followed behind him. 'Travellers!' I kept saying, knowing it was annoying him no end.

I was amazed at my granda's skill at gutting a fish. Then he even fried it for our tea. 'Where did you learn that, Granda?'

'We live beside a river, son. I was always fishing when I was a boy. My daddy taught me how to prepare a fish, and I passed it on to my son –' He stopped suddenly, remembering someone he refused to remember; maybe remembering a day long ago when he had fished with his son, my father. A day just like today.

He shook the memory away as if he were swatting a fly. 'I've not got a son.' He smiled at me. 'You're my son. Nothing, nobody in between, eh?'

I had never tasted anything as delicious as that fish. And when we'd eaten we carried our cups of tea out on to the veranda and took in the stupendous view up and down the river.

'If we had a boat,' Granda said softly, 'we could go anywhere, you and me, son.'

I watched one of the tugs head down the river towards the open sea. If only we were on that boat, sailing off to where no one would ever find us. From here, I could see the lay-by where the vans of the travellers were parked, their lights warm and welcoming. I pointed them out to my granda. 'Look, there're those travellers, down there.'

It was the wrong thing to say. It only started the whole thing up again. 'Tinkers!'

A sudden awful thought came to me. 'Granda! What if they tell the police we're here?'

'Not a chance! They'll keep well back from the police. They're never wanted anywhere, and they get moved on wherever they go. They'll not get involved with the police, don't you worry about that.'

I hoped he was right.

During those next few days I learned so much about my granda I didn't know. He seemed to have talents that he had hidden from me before. We caught more fish. He claimed to know what berries to pick and eat, and the name of almost every bird who called out through the trees. 'Since when did you become David Attenborough?'

'I'm a fount of information,' he told me. Of course, he could be making it all up. He could tell me anything, what would I know?

My granda seemed so much better here; not as vague. As if this had given him a new lease of life. He still got confused – he tried to microwave his shoe one night instead of a bowl of soup and he insisted Humphrey Bogart had got shot in our bathroom.

But it wasn't happening so often.

At night, when I settled myself in my bed, I could hear my granda muttering away as if someone was in the room with him. His favourite film star usually. John Wayne popped in regularly! But, more often than not, it was my granny.

'Ach, Bella,' I heard him say on that last night, 'what have I come to giving so much trouble to our Rory?'

So I passed my own prayers up to the Big Man. 'Are You hearing him, God? You tell my granny he's not any bother at all. We're having a great time.'

And we were. How I wished we could stay here, secluded, alone, forever.

But I knew that soon they would come looking for us and we'd be on the run again. And I hadn't a clue where to go next.

It came next day, just after tea when my granda was snoring along the seats – a text message from Darren.

THEY NO WHERE U R. THEYR CUMING. RUN.

17

'We've got to go, Granda!' I shook him awake, motioned to him to put in his hearing aid. 'They know where we are.'

I didn't have to explain who 'they' were. I had seldom seen my granda move so fast. He was trying so hard not to panic, it was almost funny.

'Get my bag! Get my pills!'

'Got 'em!' I was already stuffing all our things into our rucksacks.

My granda was at the door. 'I'm ready!' he said.

I sat him down again. 'Shoes, Granda.' I began slipping them on his feet. 'And your coat. And your scarf.' I wrapped it tightly round his neck, buttoned him up tight. When he was ready I double-checked that I had everything he would need. His medicines, that was the number-one priority. Some food, warm clothes. Every second my ears were cocked for the sound of a police siren. Surely not so soon. It would take at least half an hour to get here from the town, but still there was no time to waste.

I took one last look around the caravan. How I wished we could have stayed here. Away from the world, away from everything. Outside, it was cold and dark. Unknown. I didn't know where we were going.

Anywhere, away from here. Anywhere was safer than here now. I took my granda's hand and pulled at him. 'Come on, Granda. Time to go.' I flung my phone into the undergrowth, it was no use to me now, nowhere to charge it up, anyway.

My mind was in turmoil as we walked down the long, winding road. My eyes searched the darkness for any sign of police or social workers or even Mrs Foley. I imagined her lurking in the bushes with a butterfly net, waiting to catch us.

My granda tugged at me. 'Where are we going, son?' I looked at him, and in the moonlight his features had a blue, silvery sheen, but his eyes were full of trust. He was relying on me, and I couldn't let him down. Though I hadn't a clue where we could go now, I wouldn't let my granda know that.

'Somewhere safe, Granda,' I said, and I meant it.

'What was that?' I was talking to myself. Granda couldn't hear a word I said, and couldn't hear what I had – the distant hum of a car heading towards us on the curving road.

This soon? They must have broken the speed limit to get here.

My granda still hadn't heard it. He was talking away in his too-loud voice.

'We'll just go back to our flat. It's a free country. They can't stop us.'

Now, there was an idea. We could board ourselves up, hold each other hostage. But for how long?

'Sssh!' I pulled him to a halt, put my fingers to my

lips to silence him. 'They're coming.'

I could hear my granda begin to pant, his eyes blinked in panic. I pulled him into the bushes at the side of the path, almost hauling him off his feet.

We crouched in the undergrowth and watched as the car, a police car, zoomed past us heading for the caravan.

Granda squeezed my hand. 'I feel just like that Humphrey Bogart escaping from the Nazis.'

Here he went with the Humphrey Bogart stories again. My granda grinned at me. 'Exciting, isn't it?'

I held my breath until the car had disappeared round a bend. No siren. Of course, they wanted to catch us unawares. I gave the car two fingers. 'Too smart for you this time!' I said softly. 'Come on, we've got to get going.'

I took my granda's hand and led him back on to the road. I tried to get him to hurry, if hurry was what you could call Granda's shuffling gait. I could hear him wheeze with the effort. But I couldn't think about that. My mind was working at warp speed, thinking up a plan. If we could make the main road, the pier, perhaps we could catch a boat, a steamer heading for the islands. Or a train, taking us to the big city where we might be able to lose ourselves.

If we could just make the main road.

I kept my ears strained, listening for the returning car, imagining a whole army of police spread out and searching for us through the woods.

We were almost on the road when I heard the police

car behind us, coming back down, going slowly. They would know we hadn't gone far: the bulb in the lamp still hot to the touch, the caravan still warm from the gas fire.

I yanked my granda back into the bushes. As the car passed us I felt a single glimmer of hope. They would go back to town, report that we had left the caravan, then come back with a search party, looking for us.

Instead, the car stopped right at the entrance to the park, blocking any other vehicle from coming in, or going out.

We were so close I could hear the police radio, though its message was garbled and incoherent.

Granda was getting excited. 'It's not going away!' he said it too loud.

'Ssh!' I begged him. But why wasn't the car going?

I didn't have to wait too long to find out. Minutes later another two police cars arrived on the scene. Reinforcements.

All this for a boy and his granda? I almost stepped from cover I was so angry. I wanted to yell at them: 'Haven't you got anything better to do with your time? Haven't you got real criminals to arrest, drug dealers, murderers!'

Why couldn't they let us be?

My granda was puzzled too. 'Maybe they think you've kidnapped me.'

His voice was quivering with cold. He couldn't stay out here all night. What was I going to do?

'You run, son,' he said softly. 'You go. I'll go back. That should keep them happy.' He meant it too. It wasn't a line from one of his old movies.

'No, Granda, we're a team.' I squeezed his hand. We would either go back together, or escape together.

Together.

There was no other way.

The police were being given orders by the one in charge. I didn't have to wait long to find out what those orders were.

They began to spread out, in all directions. Some of them heading straight for us.

There was nowhere for us to run. Run? Granda could hardly walk.

I almost screamed as a hand was clamped round my mouth. They'd come up from behind. We were caught!

I was pulled round to face the man I had met that day at the loch. His eyes warned me to be quiet and he gestured to another man who had his hand clamped over my granda's mouth.

'You need to get away.' Not a question. A statement. As if he knew all about me and my granda. He nodded towards the approaching policemen. 'From them.'

His voice was so soft I could hardly hear him. 'Come with us, then. We're going to help you.'

18

I couldn't believe it at first. What was happening? Yet the determination in the man's face made me move instinctively after him.

My granda wasn't so trusting. He began to struggle, rustling the bushes. I was so afraid he would alert the police moving ever closer. I reached out to him, clutched his hand. 'It's OK, Granda. Follow me.'

I could tell by the alarm in his eyes that he still wasn't sure, but he stopped struggling and, as I talked to him softly, he allowed himself to be led down through the trees and the bushes.

How did these men know there was a pathway here? But they were expert at moving silently, avoiding branches and holes in the ground. I couldn't help looking back, sure the long arm of the law would reach out and grab us by the collar. Then I would glance at my granda. He didn't understand what was happening. I could read that in his eyes. Panicked thoughts just chased themselves round my head. Did these men mean us harm? Was I doing the right thing? Or was I leading my granda into even more danger?

At last the trees opened out on to the road, and there waiting for us were a caravan and a large camper van. Not so plush as Darren's mum's; a little battered, a little old. The door of the camper van opened and light flooded out; warm welcoming light. The boy, Tyrone, reached out a hand. 'C'mon!' he ordered.

Ever so gently, the two men helped my granda into the caravan. I jumped in behind him and Tyrone pulled the door shut.

My granda fell back on a seat, his eyes closed. Exhaustion was etched in every line of his face. I poked into my rucksack and raked through it for his pills.

'Here, I'll get him some water,' a woman said.

Without hesitation Tyrone explained, 'That's my mother.'

I took the water, pressed the pills between Granda's lips, forced him to drink. I didn't say a word to anyone until I saw his breathing become easier. This van was so unlike Darren's mum's. Brightly covered shawls were thrown over the seats, and the lamps threw out a soft and warm, orange glow. And the smell . . . it was of spices and cinnamon and garlic. It was as if we had been catapulted into another world. I felt the caravan move off, but all I could think of was my granda. Finally, he opened his eyes and smiled at me. 'That was exciting, eh?'

I gave him a punch. 'That was exciting! I nearly had a heart attack, old man!'

Only then did I turn to Tyrone and his mother and ask, 'What are you helping us for?'

The woman, Tyrone's mother, busied herself making a cup of tea. 'The police would have got you if we hadn't.'

My granda was defiant. 'You were taking a chance. We could be hardened criminals for all you know.'

Tyrone giggled. 'You two? You've got to be joking!'

'But you don't know anything about us. Why should you help us?' I asked.

'Don't know anything about you?' Tyrone said. 'You're famous, don't you know that? You've been on the telly every night. Rory McIntosh and his grand-father, on the run. Get in touch. We only want to help.' He sneered at that. 'They want to help! I don't think. They want to lock you up, more like.'

Tyrone's mother folded Granda's hands round a steaming mug of tea. 'We figured it was you two that my man met that day. Decided if you needed help, we'd help you.'

It was Granda who asked the question: 'But why should the likes of you help us?'

I held my breath. Please, Big Man, don't let him call them 'tinkers'!

He went on. 'I mean, I wasn't very nice to your man the other day.'

The woman shrugged. 'We're used to that. Any-way –' she nodded towards me – 'it was the boy we were thinking about. Same age as my Tyrone.'

She gazed at him fondly, and Tyrone grinned back like an idiot.

'Every place we stop we have social workers in, checking he's getting his education, that we're not battering lumps out of him every night. People like us can't love children, obviously!' Her voice sounded bitter, as if she was remembering arguments, confrontations from the past.

Tyrone burst in too. 'Every time we stop I get this terrible feeling that they're going to take me away from my mum and dad.'

I looked at Tyrone and saw myself and all my fears reflected in his face. The same under the skin.

'I'd die before I'd let that happen,' I told him.

Tyrone nodded. 'So would I.'

'Famous, you say?' My granda caught up with the conversation at last. 'On the telly every night?'

He sat up and took a long sip of tea. 'I hope they used a good photo of me.'

'It was both of you actually,' the woman said. 'A holiday photo, I think. You looked a lot younger then, let me tell you. Kind of handsome too, eh?'

My granda beamed. One compliment and she had him round her little finger. I looked at Tyrone, raised my eyes in exasperation.

It seemed as if my granda had found a kindred spirit.

'Call me Ruby, by the way,' she said.

Tyrone looked at her proudly. 'My dad calls her his "jewel".'

Ruby laughed loudly. 'He calls me a lot of other names as well.' She switched off the lamp, and leaned down to look out of the window and her eyes skimmed the road. 'Better keep quiet, eh? Softly does it.'

I moved beside her and looked out through the netted curtain. Sammy had started up the van and we were passing the entrance to the caravan site. Three police cars barred the way, and there were a few policeman standing around. All I could see were men in uniform, their faces blank. They were coming after us and they wouldn't stop till they caught us. My granda was right: we were on the run, and they could have been Nazis. My heart missed a beat as I noticed them glance at the vans as they purred past. Then their attention was turned once more to someone calling in the undergrowth.

I didn't stop watching until we turned the corner on the moonlit coast road and the police cars were lost to sight.

Safe.

For now at least.

19

I woke next morning to the smell of bacon frying,
and the sound of pop music on the radio. I sat up
quickly, not quite remembering where I was. It took
me a moment to put my thoughts together and
remember the traumatic events of last night –
Darren's text message, running from the police, and
the surprising intervention of Tyrone's family.

Was that only last night?

My granda was still sleeping, snoring quietly in the
pull-down bed beside me. The van wasn't moving and
when I drew aside the curtain I saw that we were in
yet another lay-by, this time a good distance from the
road.

Ruby popped her head round the door and smiled.
'Let your grandfather sleep. You come and have some
breakfast.'

Breakfast sounded good, smelled even better. I slid
from the bed, careful not to wake Granda. In the
kitchen-cum-living room, Tyrone's dad was sitting
drinking tea. 'Mornin',' he said gruffly and he
motioned me to take a seat.

'Morning,' I replied.

Ruby put a roll filled with crusty bacon in front of
me and I bit into it hungrily. I hadn't realized just

how famished I was. 'This is awful good of you,' I said, spluttering crumbs all over the place.

Tyrone's dad shrugged and nodded to Ruby. 'Thank her. She's the softie in the family.'

She threw back her head and laughed loudly. 'Don't you believe a word of that, Rory. This man of mine, this Sammy, he cries at soppy films. He can't resist kittens. That advert with the tiny pup and the toilet paper? He sobs at that one. He's the one that says, "Oh, we can't leave them there. We've got to help." As if we don't have enough trouble with the police.'

'Oh, I don't want us to cause you any trouble with the police.'

Sammy glared at Ruby. 'Ach, don't listen to the woman. She's a trouble-maker, like most women.'

This only made Ruby laugh even more. 'I'd like to see you do without a woman. You big useless lump of lard.'

At that, Sammy tried to give her a smack on the bottom but she dodged it and walloped him with her tea towel instead. But they were both laughing. 'What a way to talk to the head of the family. Eh, Rory? What's the world coming to?'

Ruby found that even funnier. 'The head of the family! You know who the boss is in this family. So eat up and then get on with your work.'

Sammy pretended to be scared. 'Yes, boss,' he winked at me.

'I'm sorry my granda wasn't very nice to you the other day.'

I blushed at the memory of it.

Sammy waved that aside. 'Ach, he's an old man. My pa was the same. He was an old ba –'

Ruby waved a warning finger at him. 'Language, Sammy!'

'An old bandit. I was going to say he was an old bandit.'

At that very moment, my very own 'old bandit' appeared at the door, bleary-eyed. 'Do I smell bacon? Where am I? How did I get here?'

I jumped up and helped him to a chair. 'What question do you want answered first?'

My granda eyed Sammy suspiciously. Sammy held his stare. 'Aye, it's me, old man. The tinker.'

I almost died of embarrassment. My granda sputtered with indignation. 'I didn't say that. Tell them, Rory. I didn't call him a tinker, did I?'

Sammy lifted the paper and pretended to study it. 'My name's Sammy if you're interested.'

I could see my granda still hadn't come round to Sammy, but Ruby had him twisted round her finger. She put a hand on his shoulder. 'Do you fancy a bacon roll, handsome?'

His eyes lit up. 'That would be lovely, sweetheart,' he said.

Sammy glanced up at him. 'Sweetheart, is it? That's my wife, you know.'

'Aye, and you're lucky to have her.'

I was going to faint. My granda doesn't care! But Ruby only laughed. 'You tell him, Granda.'

It was then I noticed that he was ready to bite into his bacon roll without his teeth. 'Granda! Where're your teeth?'

'They're in my pocket,' he said.

Oh no, I hated it when he put them in his pocket. That would mean they would be covered with bits of fluff and goodness knows what else.

I was washing them at the sink when Tyrone appeared. I'd assumed he'd gone to school, but he was carrying eggs and potatoes and told me at once he'd been to the nearby farm. 'Mister Harrison says we can stay here for a couple of days if we want. We've been here before,' he explained to me. 'My dad does odd jobs for him. He's really handy, my dad.'

Sammy put his paper down. 'That's good of him, but we're moving off tomorrow. Up north. We've got family up there. It's your cousin's birthday.' He turned to me. 'It would be safer for you as well. As far away from here as possible.'

Ruby chipped in. 'The other caravan went another way. They've gone south just in case we'd been followed.'

They'd gone to all this trouble, for us?

Tyrone jumped and switched on the television. 'Have you seen yourselves? You're famous.'

The news came on and, though we still hadn't made the national headlines, we were the top story on the Scottish news.

The boy and his grandfather on the run.

Val Jessup appeared on the screen looking even

94

younger than she did in life, pleading with us if we were watching to get in touch. We were in no trouble. The authorities were only worried about us both, especially my granda, whose health was a real concern.

Granda was alerted to the news when Darren's mum appeared on the screen. 'How did that baggage get on there?' he shouted. Too loud. He didn't have his hearing aid in again, so he couldn't hear a word she was saying. Ruby switched it on to subtitles for him.

He ranted all through her piece. 'Look at her! Loves being on television. Thinks she's a film star.'

Darren's mum had obviously had her hair done, and her make-up. She did look pretty. Even I had to admit that.

She also spoke in a very posh voice. 'It was my son, Darren, who gave the keys of my caravan to Rory, his best friend. He didn't mean any harm. Thought he was doing the right thing. Of course, as soon as I realized the spare key was missing, I knew what had happened.' She paused for effect, glanced to the side and nodded as if she was receiving directions. 'I deduced that Darren had given Rory the key so they could hide out there.' She paused again, as if she were waiting for applause, or as if she had just revealed the identity of Jack the Ripper.

My granda started again. 'She deduced! Who does she think she is? Sherlock blinkin' Holmes!'

At that she moved closer to the camera and her

voice changed. Now it was *her* voice and it sounded so sincere: 'Come back, son. Bring your granda. He can't take this. He's not well. You know that. You've got to come back.'

Was she right? Was I doing more harm than good? I sat back in my seat and felt my insides freeze as if I had swallowed a mouthful of ice-cold porridge.

On the screen came the photograph. Me and my granda, two summers ago, at Edinburgh Castle. Smiling, happy. It seemed an age away now.

My granda suddenly pounded the table. 'I'm never going back,' he roared. 'I'd rather die of cold and hunger, and be free!'

20

*N*ext morning we were on the move again, travelling north through the lush countryside of Perthshire. We didn't use the motorway, but turned on to the country roads. 'ALTERNATIVE TOURIST ROUTE' the sign said.

'Is that because of us?' I asked Tyrone.

'No, my pa always uses these roads. You find better places to stop. My pa knows all the best places.' He said it proudly.

'It must be exciting, like having a new adventure every day,' I said.

'It is. I love it.'

'Tell me somebody who wouldn't?' It was a boy's dream life, I thought. No ties, no school, just adventure.

'My sister for one,' Tyrone said as if he still couldn't believe it. 'She ran away to go and stay with my auntie. In a house!' He added that in an even more incredulous tone.

'Is she daft?' I asked him.

'Got it in one, Rory,' Tyrone laughed.

Even Granda seemed to be enjoying himself sitting in the front of the van enjoying the view. Listening to us.

'Tyrone,' I said, 'how did you get a name like that?'

My granda jumped into the conversation, about the only thing he could jump into these days. 'He was called after a film star!' he said.

'He was not!' I almost shouted. 'According to you everybody is called after a film star. I suppose I was as well.'

'Indeed you were. Rory Calhoun.'

'Rory Calhoun! I never heard of him. You make things up as you go along, Granda.'

Granda almost went blue in the face. 'See you, boy. You take it out of me, so you do. Talking to me like that.'

'And what about you? I suppose you were called after some film star as well.'

He answered without hesitation. 'Aye, I was. I was called after . . .' He paused. 'What's my name again?'

Now this is worrying stuff when it happens to your own granda. 'You're really losing it, old man. What's your name? You don't even know your name!'

'Well, no wonder. All you ever call me is Granda! Granda this, and Granda that. Everybody calls me Granda. It's no wonder I've forgotten my name.'

'Daft old bat!' I muttered under my breath.

'Wait till you get to my age, boy, if you ever live that long!'

I looked at Tyrone. 'Another pointless conversation with my granda, Tyrone.'

But Tyrone was laughing, and so was his dad, as if

we were saying something funny. Suddenly my granda started laughing too.

He was warming now to Sammy; hadn't called him a tinker once. And as for Ruby, he thought she was marvellous. He was always admiring her legs, or her ruby lips.

'Hey, that's my woman!' Sammy would warn him and Ruby would retort, 'You leave Granda be. I love getting compliments from good-looking men.'

And as we drove through tiny villages, little newsagents had posters outside with newspaper headlines about Granda and me. Everyone seemed to be looking for us.

That worried me. 'You'll get into trouble if they find out you helped us,' I said.

'Why should we?' Sammy asked me. 'We haven't kidnapped you. And you're not escaped convicts. It's a free country. You can go where you please.'

I knew we couldn't stay with them forever, though the idea was appealing. It wouldn't be fair.

But just for the moment, I let it be. I was enjoying myself. But there was one thing I could help with.

When we stopped that afternoon, I handed Ruby some money.

'What's that for?' she asked.

'You can't feed us for nothing.' I pushed it towards her, tried to stuff the notes into her fist.

Her face grew hard. 'For all you eat. Mind you, that old man could eat for Britain!' She nodded to where Granda was sitting on a stool outside the caravan, getting stuck into a bowl of her homemade soup. He was slurping and sloshing and grinding and gnashing. A sure sign he was enjoying it.

Her hand closed round mine. 'Keep the money, Rory. You're going to need it. But it's a sad day when someone can't lend a helping hand without getting paid for it.'

I was touched; embarrassed now by all the times I had slammed the door on travellers when they would come selling their wares.

I confessed all this to Tyrone later. 'See, we're not all bad. Some of us are really nice. Not all of us, though.' He spoke like an old, worldly wise man. 'They're the ones get us all a bad name. But then, there's plenty of people give you a bad name too and you don't judge everybody by them, do you?'

It was true, but I promised myself then that I'd never judge anyone again.

'We're going to have a brilliant night tonight,' Tyrone said. 'A party.'

'A party?'

'We're going to meet up with my pa's brother and his family. Up in Forfar. We know a good place there.'

I stiffened. 'A whole family, and they know about us?'

Tyrone shrugged. 'Of course they do. He's my uncle. Totally trustworthy.' He seemed to think about that. 'Even if he has been in the jail for stealing.'

I almost fell off my seat and Tyrone laughed loudly. 'Only kidding. Keep your Y-fronts on.'

The other family were already there when we reached the outskirts of Forfar. Dusk was falling and the door of their caravan lay open and the warm glow from the lamps inside soaked the grass. The two families greeted each other warmly. Sammy's brother, a man as tall as Sammy, had a wild, black beard that made him look as if he'd had an electric shock. His wife wasn't half as pretty as Ruby. She had fair hair that hung around her shoulders and she was wearing wellies of all things.

'Is that the fashion?' I whispered to Tyrone.

Tyrone whispered back. 'I've never seen her without them. I think she was born wearing them.'

A skinny stick of a girl came towards us balancing a baby on her hip. She looked so like the woman she must have been her daughter, except her hair was shiny and cut close against her head.

'Oh look, Joshua, it's your cousin Tyrone,' she said to the baby. Joshua immediately began to cry. 'Now see what you've done!' she snapped at Tyrone.

Tyrone clamped his hands over my eyes. 'Don't look at her ugly face, Rory. You'll turn to stone.'

'I beg your pardon. I'm considered pretty,' she said.

'Yeah, pretty ugly.'

'Is she your girlfriend, Tyrone?' I asked him

At that, both of them pretended to be sick on the ground. 'I would have to be mad, blind or desperate!' Tyrone snorted.

'Two out of three's not bad.' The girl looked at me then. 'My name's Zara, since it doesn't look as if I'm going to be introduced. And you must be the famous Rory McIntosh.'

Did everyone know me? It seemed so. The man, Zara's father, was called Bernie and he came over all smiles to introduce himself and his wife. 'I see you've met Zara,' he said. 'And Joshua. Say hello to Rory, Joshua.'

I felt a bit silly talking to Joshua but I did it anyway. Granda, however, talked to him as if he were his best friend.

'We know all about you, Granda,' Bernie said. 'They're widening the net looking for you. You're going to have to think about what you're going to do next.'

'Rory and me have plans, isn't that right, son?'

Did we? It was the first I'd heard about it.

'Well, time to talk about all that later,' Sammy said, slipping an arm round my granda's shoulders. 'For tonight, we're just going to enjoy ourselves.'

21

*B*ernie brought out his guitar and began to play even before we'd finished eating the sausages and the mash and the beans that were Zara's chosen birthday feast.

'Do you know this one, Granda?' he said, and he started to pluck out the tune of 'Ten Guitars'. I knew it because my granda had it on an old record.

'"Ten Guitars"!' my granda shouted. 'It's brilliant!' And he began to sing. Well, what passed for singing. He didn't know the words either, so he just made them up as he went along.

'He does that all the time,' I moaned to Tyrone.

It took no time at all for my granda to get into the party mood. After 'Ten Guitars', he wanted something called 'Do Not Forsake Me, Oh, My Darling'.

'It'll be from some old film,' I said. 'Every song he knows is from some old film.'

To my surprise, Bernie knew it and plucked it out expertly on his guitar. Sammy and Ruby knew it too and they sang along with Granda.

After that, one song followed another. Bernie sang some rousing Irish melody, and Sammy serenaded Ruby with a love song.

'I think that's bootiful,' my granda said with a tear in his eye.

Me and Tyrone thought it was embarrassing.

Then Ruby pulled my granda to his feet. 'What about a dance now?' she said.

They danced around a circle with the warm glow from the caravans illuminating the grass and the music drifting up into the starlit sky.

I watched my granda as he danced. He was happy. It had been such a long time since I'd seen him this happy . . . or carefree. I knew then that no matter what the future held for us, I'd done the right thing taking him away.

Granda was exhausted when the dance finished and he collapsed into a chair beside me.

'I've not lost my touch,' he said.

'No, just your breath,' I replied, but he ignored me.

'I always was a good dancer.'

'You were stepping all over Ruby's toes,' I told him. I could see Ruby limping into the van.

My granda leaned closer and his voice was low. 'She's a lovely lass, but she's not a dancer.'

Honestly, he is unbelievable!

Everybody got a turn to sing at the party. Me and Tyrone did a rap song together. Definitely the best turn of the night, even though we were booed off. The rest of them were just too old to appreciate good music. Of course, there were lots of 'ooos' and 'ahhhs' when Zara sang some daft girlie song.

'You're the only one who hasn't given us a song, Ruby,' my granda said.

Ruby shook her head. 'I don't sing, Granda,' she said.

Bernie said, 'No, Ruby's party piece is to tell fortunes, she's got the gift.'

She stepped across to my granda. 'Want me to see what the future holds for you, Granda?' she asked.

'Who? Me? At my age? As long as my name doesn't appear in the death notices in the paper tomorrow I'll be quite content, sweetheart.' He looked over at me. 'But the boy there, tell him his future.' Then he smiled with a cheeky grin. 'He's got a great one. This boy's special. Nobody like him in all the world.'

'OK,' I said to Ruby. 'What have I got to do, cross your palm with silver?'

She sat on a stool beside me and took my hand in hers. She caressed my palm ever so gently, then folded her hand round mine and closed her eyes.

She began to breathe so deeply I thought she had fallen asleep. I glanced at my granda and he was watching, fascinated. Her voice was low when she began to speak. 'I'm not telling you anything you don't know already when I say there are people after you. They're closing in.'

'Will they catch us?' I asked her eagerly.

Her eyes opened, and her gaze warmed me. 'No. They won't catch you, Rory.'

I gave a thumbs-up sign to my granda.

Ruby carried on, her voice low. 'They won't find

you. It's you who will go to them. You won't have any choice.'

I shook my head. 'Never.'

I wouldn't let that happen. There was no way ever I would give myself up.

She smiled. 'But not yet. You still have many adventures to come. Adventures, that's how I see your life. As an adventure.'

'Me and my granda, we'll always be together, won't we?'

I wanted her to say that we'd find an island and live there, forever.

'You will meet people who will help you. And there will be people you can't trust. You're looking for something, Rory, and when you find it, everything changes for you.' She drew in her breath sharply as if something had pained her. Her voice was even softer. 'And a terrible sadness will come first.'

'A terrible sadness,' I repeated. I didn't like the sound of that.

Ruby shook her head. 'Because of that terrible sadness, Rory, you will find the thing you're looking for.'

But I wasn't looking for anything, I wanted to tell her.

She pushed my hand against me and I saw that there were tears in her eyes. 'Is my granda going to be OK, Ruby?'

She didn't get a chance to answer that. My granda did. 'Of course, I'm going to be OK! I'm made of good stuff. By the way, are we getting any tea at this party?'

So the mood changed again and tea was brought out and more sausages and the dancing and the singing went on into the night.

It was only later as I lay in bed next to my granda that I remembered that Ruby never had answered my question: 'Is my granda going to be OK?'

22

*T*yrone was shaking me awake. 'Rory, come and see this!' I rubbed my eyes and threw the covers from me. Granda was still snoring – and this is the man who says he can't sleep!

Tyrone was pulling at me. 'Come on!'

'What's the panic?' I followed him into the kitchen area. Ruby was standing, holding a tea towel to her face. She glanced at me as I came in, then looked back at the television. My eyes were drawn to it. And there was me, my photo filling the screen.

'The missing pair were last seen at the caravan park, and it would appear that travellers were in the area at that time. It seems now that they left at the same time as the last sighting of Mister McIntosh and his grandson. We urge these people to get in touch. They are in no trouble. They just need to be eliminated from our enquiries.'

Ruby snorted. 'Eliminated from our enquiries! You'd think they were searching for a couple of serial killers.'

The voice went on: 'I have to reiterate that no one is in any trouble here. We are only concerned for the safety and well-being of Mister McIntosh and his grandson.'

I flopped on to a seat. 'They'll be looking for you now.'

Ruby didn't argue with that. 'They'll find us,' was all she said.

'Me and my granda'll have to go.'

'No!' Tyrone looked at his mum. 'They don't, do they? We could hide them if they do come looking. Just say we've never seen them.'

It all seemed so simple to Tyrone.

Ruby smiled at him. 'No, son. It's time for them to move on.' She said it as if she knew something I didn't, and I remembered her fortune from last night. More adventures, and a terrible sadness.

A terrible sadness. I didn't want to think about that.

Tyrone was tugging at my sleeve, pointing back at the television. 'Hey look, Rory, they're talking to people in the street about you.'

The interviewer was asking people what they thought of the old man who was on the run with his grandson. The first woman had no sympathy at all.

'If that old man had any sense he'd bring the laddie back home. He's missing school, and goodness knows what terrible things could happen to him.'

That made me laugh. 'She doesn't know my granda, does she? He hasn't got any sense at all.'

But if she had no sympathy, everyone else made up for her.

'I think it's wonderful!' one man said. 'They don't want to be split up, so what choice did they have?'

'Leave them be. Let them live and die together. They've not done anything wrong.'

'We've got criminals, gun culture, drugs, and what are the police doing? Tracking down an old man and a young boy! Wasting police time.'

Ruby smiled at me. 'You're becoming something of a *cause célèbre*,' she said.

'A cause . . . what?'

She grinned. 'People are taking sides about you, arguing about the rights and wrongs of your case. That's good. The more people who know your plight, the better chance you have of staying together.'

We got Granda up and dressed and, once I'd found his hearing aid (stuffed into a smelly sock), I explained to him that we were going to have to leave. I thought he'd argue about that. He was comfortable here. He loved Ruby. But maybe because of that, not wanting to cause them harm, he said he was eager to get back on the road.

'Not today?' Tyrone actually sounded disappointed.

'Aye,' my granda insisted.

I didn't want to leave them either. Where would we go? 'Up north,' I suggested. Remote and wild, no one would ever find us there, surely?

Bernie and Sammy didn't agree. 'Too remote, Rory. Granda would never survive sleeping rough in this weather.' They had a better idea. 'We have family in Glasgow. You get there, by train. They'll meet you at Queen Street Station. Give you shelter till you move on. Give you time to think.'

'We'll drive you to Dundee, and you can get a train from there.'

But we were famous now. People knew our faces. They'd be looking for us.

My granda had an answer to that. 'We could go in disguise. I could be your granny.' He put on a simpering female voice that didn't sound like any granny I'd ever met. 'And you could be my lovely granddaughter, Morag.'

I looked at him as if he was mad – which he was. 'I am not dressing up as a lassie for you.'

'I'm willing to dress up as a granny. Ruby will lend me one of her frocks, and a bit of lipstick and Bob's your uncle.'

'Or, in this case, your granny.' Tyrone laughed.

'It's OK for you, Granda. When you get old, men and women look the same. Women grow moustaches. Look at Mrs Foley. But me? I could never pass for a girl.'

Tyrone understood. 'I'm with you there, bro'.'

'A frock would be an improvement,' Zara said, listening at the door with Joshua in her arms.

Ruby came up with the best solution. 'Just travel separately. Sit in different carriages, bury your head in a book. I bet no one will notice you.'

'And head south after Glasgow,' Sammy said. 'You're only on the news up here, for the moment. No one will know who you are in England.'

Ruby filled a flask with her homemade minestrone soup, and packed cheese and chicken sandwiches into my rucksack. I could see she was almost crying the whole time.

'I wish you didn't have to go,' Tyrone said. 'I was beginning to get used to you.'

'I wish we didn't have to go either,' I said truthfully. 'Couldn't your mum and dad adopt us?'

They drove us to Dundee, and it was harder than I could imagine to say goodbye. Had we only met them a few days ago? I felt they were family now. I cared about them, and they cared about me and my granda.

At the station, Ruby hugged him so tight I waited for the sound of his old bones cracking, but he didn't seem to mind.

Sammy handed me a slip of paper. 'That's my mobile number. If you ever need anything – anything – you call me. You promise?'

Ruby held me for a long time. 'My cousin will be there to meet you. Let me know you're OK, will you?'

I felt sick as I watched them drive off, sick and alone. Then I looked around and realized that I really was alone. My granda had disappeared.

I ran inside the station and found him staring at the timetable, but he didn't fool me. He didn't have his glasses on and, anyway, he couldn't have read a thing through his tears. I squeezed his hand. 'You liked them, didn't you, Granda?'

He didn't look at me. He just stared at the board with the tears trickling down his face. 'I'll never call them tinkers again, Rory.'

23

*W*e didn't sit together on the train. Sammy had bought our two tickets, one way, to Glasgow and I slipped one of them into Granda's hand on the platform. I tried my best to get him to understand he had to sit in another carriage, but he was having none of it. It was just as well, really – it was better that I keep my eye on him. So I motioned him to a seat as far away from me as possible and I pretended to be really interested in a *Big Issue* magazine someone had left behind.

The whole journey my granda kept looking up at me, checking I was still there, grinning at me. He looked for all the world like a forlorn mongrel I'd forgotten to feed.

'Don't keep looking,' I kept praying. 'Someone will notice and put two and two together, or rather, put me and my granda together.'

But, Ruby had been right, no one seemed interested in me or my granda. The carriage was filled with commuters, men in suits talking loudly on their mobile phones, women with briefcases poring over papers on their tables. A boy in a back-to-front baseball cap slugging lemonade out of a bottle. A mother with a crying baby. People returning from shopping trips to the city.

Then I spotted her; squashed into a window seat. At first I thought they'd let a horse into the carriage by mistake. She was a dead ringer for one. Her big horsey eyes were staring at me. I snapped the magazine back over my face. But when I risked a look a moment later she was still watching. Then her eyes moved down the carriage, towards my granda. To my horror, he was watching me and when our eyes met, what did he do? He grinned at me again! I knew the game was up then. She had us sussed. I could almost see the wheels in her head working everything out. *Seen that boy somewhere, but where? And that daft-looking old man looks familiar too? Hey, he's smiling at the boy! They know each other. It's THEM!*

I couldn't help but look back at her. Her eyes had gone wide. I tried to look unconcerned but my brain was going into overdrive! We had to get off this train.

The next stop was Perth, and already people were standing, pulling on coats, hauling briefcases and bags from overhead shelves. Granda was still looking at me. He hadn't a clue where we were going. He was waiting for my cue.

But get off at Perth? We had bought tickets straight through to Glasgow. But it wasn't worth the risk. Now her eyes were darting between us. Any moment now, the ticket collector would come round and she would tell him who we were. I stood up. The woman jerked straight in her seat. Even from the corner of my eye I could see that. I pushed through the crowd. She couldn't get out, trapped as she was in a window seat.

I prayed she was too much of a lady to start shouting after me.

She must have lost sight of me as I weaved my way down the carriage to my granda. 'Is that us now?' he asked as I helped him to his feet.

I didn't answer. I wanted to be the first to step on to the platform. Already a crowd was there waiting, ready to push in for a seat. With any luck we could get lost in the surge of people getting out and getting on.

By myself, I could run. Up the steps and over the bridge, and out into the street. But my granda couldn't run. He had enough trouble walking.

I didn't dare look back at the woman. Was she still watching us? Was she right behind me, her arm almost touching my shoulder? But, as we made our way up the steps, the train began to move off and, when I looked, no one was chasing us, shouting our names, trying to stop us.

However, the chances were that she would alert someone on the train and they would get word back to this station. We still needed to get as far away from here as possible.

'I'll have to go to the toilet, son,' my granda said as we went out of the station. He shuffled into the gents. I just hoped it wasn't his blinking bowels again. I could be here for ages.

I stood, stamping my feet as I waited for him in the cold, dark street. Every moment I was waiting for someone to spot me, to reach out and grab me.

Suddenly, someone did.

'I thought it was you!' The boy swung me round, kept his grip on my jacket. I had seen him before – slugging lemonade on the train. 'Where's the old man?'

I struggled, but he wouldn't let me go.

He looked around. His face was the colour of wallpaper paste. 'Your granda? Where is he?'

I tried to keep my eyes from darting towards the toilets, but I couldn't stop myself.

'Away to the lavvy, is he?' he laughed. 'I knew I recognized you on that train. Know what I'm gonny do? I'm gonny turn you two in. I'll be famous. Be on the telly.'

'We're not criminals.' My voice came out like a whimper. 'Just let us go. Please.'

He pushed me hard against a wall. 'Let you go? Are you mad? This could be my big break.'

His big break? He was talking as if he was auditioning for *Popstars*.

What was I going to do? Kick him? Bite him? Force him to let me go? My mind was a panicking jumble of plans. Then I could run to the toilets, grab my granda. We could both race down the street and out of his sight. Get away from him before he had a chance to recover, running as fast as we could . . .

And, of course, that was where the dream crashed on impact.

Granda run? A tortoise on crutches could go faster.

'Let us go! You won't even get a reward.' I tried to

plead to his better nature. Ha! That was a joke. Guys like him didn't have a better nature.

He sneered, and revealed teeth that hadn't visited a dentist in years. His breath was stinking as well. Stale smoke and Brussels sprouts if my nose didn't let me down.

'Fame will be reward enough for me,' he sneered. 'Right. He comes outta the lavvy and I take you to the cops.'

'I'm on my own. My granda stayed on the train. He's going to Glasgow. I was fed up with him anyway.'

His face came so close I felt like biting his nose. 'Your granda's too daft to go anywhere on his own. I saw him coming off the train with you, stupid. As soon as he comes here, you're nicked, pal. And he better hurry up.' He turned round to look for him – and that's when it happened. I didn't see it coming and certainly neither did Sprout Breath. A bottle was walloped right across his head. I think it was the one he had been slugging out of on the train. His eyes went wide, he let out a low whimper and then he crumpled, sinking to the ground like a pile of old clothes. Out for the count.

I gasped as my granda stepped out of the shadows, still clutching a lemonade bottle. 'Daft am I? Well, I'm not that daft.'

'Granda! You've killed him!'

My granda tutted. 'Rubbish. He's fine. Or he will be when he wakes up.'

He had a grip on my shoulders and was pulling me

on. 'Come on, we've got to make our getaway.'

'We weren't criminals before, but we are now. You've just committed grievous bodily harm.'

'We're not going to get caught.' He was stumbling so much I was sure he would fall.

'But, Granda, I don't know where to go now. And I don't know how to get there even if I did.'

I was ready to cry. I glanced back at the pavement, at the boy's limp body, and knew that was the worst thing that could have happened.

Suddenly, my granda spoke and his voice was sure and strong.

'I know where we're going,' he said, and he grabbed me again and hauled me on. 'Anywhere but here, that's where. And I know how we're going to get there.'

This was a new Granda – in command, sure of himself, for the moment at least.

'You do?' I asked him. 'How?'

'We're going to steal a car,' he said calmly.

24

'We're going to do . . . what?' He was dragging me behind him like a sack of potatoes. I was sure I must have heard him wrong. But I hadn't.

'We'll hot-wire a car. Make a run for it.'

My mouth was hanging open. I saw my future stretch ahead of me . . . in jail. He was turning me into a master criminal, and I'd done nothing wrong.

'Granda! Who do you think we are? What happened to you in that toilet? You went in a gibbering old loon and came out the Godfather! Did you have a personality transplant in there?'

I was gibbering myself, but I just couldn't take in what was happening. Finally, I made him stop. 'Granda! You whacked a guy over the head there. You might have killed him.'

He waved that away as if it was nonsense. 'Rubbish! He'll be fine when he wakes up. Anyway, it was self-defence.'

'I don't know whether the law will see it like that. And now, to make matters worse, you want to steal a car!' Suddenly another thought struck me. 'Anyway, how do you know how to hot-wire a car?'

He began dragging me on again. 'I was a motor

mechanic. I know everything there is to know about motors.'

That was true. Cars had always been his passion. I could still remember his Morris Minor, his pride and joy, and our jaunts down the coast every weekend.

'But hot-wiring's against the law, Granda.'

'We're fugitives, Rory,' he said, seriously. 'We've got to save ourselves. It's us against them. Anything goes.'

I couldn't believe this. He was talking like a character in one of his old gangster movies.

What was I going to do with him?

All the time he was talking he was pulling me on. Suddenly he stopped. 'This one'll do fine.' He nodded to an old, blue Corsa on the other side of the road.

'It's a bit old,' I complained.

'I don't know how to hot-wire a new one, daftie! Who do you think *I* am, Superman?'

His eyes searched up and down the street. 'Somebody's parked this here to get on a train. There're no houses near, nobody to see us. Are you ready?'

His tongue was hanging out and he was crouching down. His arthritis would be killing him later. But I watched him in amazement. This was a Granda I had forgotten had ever existed. He scratched around and found an old piece of wire lying on the road and he used it to open the car door and, once inside the car, he fumbled under the wheel, pulled at some wires and the next minute the engine spurted into life.

I was in a daze. 'I think you missed your vocation.'

He winked at me. 'I was always borrowing cars when I was a lad.'

I remembered then he had once told me that my dad had done the same, 'borrowing cars', so he could joyride around the town. 'Like father like son,' I said, and immediately regretted it.

He scowled at me. 'Don't have a son! Except you!'

If starting the car amazed me, his driving terrified me. That was when our real adventure began.

'Ah! You're on the wrong side of the road, Granda!'

'Granda! Don't overtake here!'

'Granda! Slow down!'

He ranted back at me. 'You're as bad as your granny. She was the worst back-seat driver that ever sat in a front seat.'

I thought we would never leave the city alive. How he didn't crash I will never understand. The Big Man must have been looking out for us again.

Finally, by some miracle, we made the back roads leading south. I didn't know where we were going. At that moment, I didn't care.

We were still free.

It was well into the afternoon when we stopped in a lay-by and my granda slept, snoring as peacefully as if he were safe and secure in his own bed. I wished I could sleep too, but my mind was full of questions. What were we going to do next? How would we get petrol without anyone catching us? And now, would the police be looking for not an innocent boy and his grandfather, but two thugs ready to use violence to keep out of the hands of the law?

In my terrified mind, I saw that boy regain consciousness. (Oh please, Big Man, let him regain consciousness.) I heard him embellishing his story so that I would have been holding him down while my granda (who would, by his account, have muscles like Arnold Schwarzenegger) assaulted him with a deadly weapon. His pipe probably.

Now, if we were caught, would we be sent to jail?

Everything seemed to be getting worse by the minute. Was it only last night that we'd slept warm and cosy in Tyrone's van?

25

Granda slept for over an hour. 'I'm hungry,' was the first thing he said. 'Have you got those sandwiches that Ruby made?'

We ate the sandwiches as if they were the finest meal a TV chef ever created. Granda spluttered enough crumbs over me to feed a family of five. And he talked all the time he ate. He could hardly keep the excitement out of his voice. It worried me a bit, that excitement. It couldn't last. And what would take its place? Exhaustion?

'We'll go south, to one of the ports. Dover. Catch a boat for France, or . . . where's that other country over there?'

'Holland,' I told him, hoping my geography was right.

'I still think we could get dressed up.'

'And where are we going to find women's clothes?' I asked him.

He had an answer for that. 'We'll steal them.'

He was getting worse by the minute. 'You *are* turning into the Godfather, old man. Grievous bodily harm, car theft, and, now, shoplifting. You're a bad influence on me. Leading your only grandson into a life of crime!'

He gave me a thump in the ribs. 'Oh belt up, or else I'll add grandson-battering to my list.'

He started rummaging about in the glove compartment. 'Is there no' a map in this car?'

There was better than a map. There was an *Atlas of the Roads of Britain*. Not only that, but a whole pile of music tapes. Nothing for me to get excited about, however. Whoever owned this car must be about the same age as my granda. And a very sad person at that. Frank Sinatra. That was all. Just Frank Sinatra.

My granda stuck one in the tape deck right away, and what was he singing?

'"My Way",'

My granda played it so often, over and over, on that journey that my eyes began to glaze over. I thought I was going to puke.

'Granda!' I yelled finally. 'Give us a break! At least let us hear the news.'

He shook his head. 'No, son. We're the news. But that song, it just lifts my heart up. That's how we're doing it. My way.'

He grinned like an idiot and the song was repeated again.

You can't fight it, I thought, so I joined in the chorus with my granda. I knew all the words by now anyway.

'I think we're going to need petrol,' my granda said, as we drove down the dark winding country roads.

'Trust you to steal a car that needs petrol.'

'Och, you ungrateful devil of a boy. I should have let you steal the car!'

My heart was in my mouth as I tried to figure out how to get the petrol safely. After all, once the car was stopped and the engine off, we couldn't exactly hot-wire a car in a crowded forecourt. We needed somewhere quiet and isolated.

At the very edge of a tiny village I saw the answer. A dimly lit petrol station loomed ahead of us. The last sign of civilization before black night took over the road again.

'There, Granda,' I said.

I would like to say he pulled to a halt silently. The truth was more of a screech. There were no other cars in the garage, and there was only a gloomy light in the office where I could see a man poring over the evening paper.

It was worth the risk, I decided. I'd quickly put petrol in, though I'd never done that before, and run into the office with the money, then belt back to the car and we would be off before the man even realized who we were.

That was the plan.

First of all, I hadn't a clue how to put petrol in. And second, I didn't even know where the petrol cap of this car was.

I bent down to look for it when suddenly I felt a tap on my shoulder.

'What do you think you're doing, son?'

I swallowed but couldn't say a word. The man behind me was thickset, and he either hadn't shaved for days, or he was working on his designer stubble. His eyes were a piercing blue, and they were piercing me now. He pointed to a sign.

I was so nervous I couldn't even read the sign. I just hoped it didn't say: 'YOU'RE NICKED'.

'My . . . my uncle . . .' I motioned towards my granda who looked as if he was nodding off again. 'He's got a bad leg. I told him to stay in the car. I'd put the petrol in . . .' I ran out of words to say. 'Sorry.'

I was trying to imagine the scene with my granda struggling out of the car and me trying to explain to him how to put petrol in. The blind leading the blind. And him with his hearing-aid batteries wearing out.

The man was shaking his head. 'No, son.' He indicated the sign again.

'WE SERVE YOU'.

He growled. 'You get back in the car and I'll fill you up.' He leaned in the window and spoke to my granda. 'Old-fashioned service.'

My granda snored in his face.

'Now, how much do you want?' His voice was harsh and he sounded hoarse. I pulled a crumpled note from my pocket. My throat was so dry that my own voice came out like a croak. 'This much.'

Then I got into the car beside my granda and panicked about how he was going to hot-wire anything with this man looking on.

My granda was no help at all. He was sound asleep! In the middle of a panic he was sound asleep!

I tried to nudge him, but he only snored in answer. Yet I had to wake him if we were going to get away.

I looked round at the man and he was putting the nozzle back in the pump. He stepped round beside my window and I handed him the money. 'Thanks, mister,' I said, as cheerily as I could. 'I'll wake up my uncle and we'll be on our way.'

The man didn't make any motion to take my money. He leaned into the car and looked at my granda, and then he looked at me. 'No, son, I don't think you'll be going anywhere tonight.'

26

*T*his was it! We'd been sussed once again. And this man was too big, too hairy, too scary, for my granda to assault. Anyway, Granda was sound asleep.

'What do you mean?' I asked him, still trying to bluff it.

Suddenly, the man grinned at me. 'Don't look so worried, son. I want to help.'

I must have looked puzzled because he went on to explain. 'Everybody's talking about you two. Looking for you. You'll not get far, even in this.' He peered into the car, at Granda's sleeping face. 'And your grandfather's tired. He looks done in.'

'But why should you help us?'

'You're not criminals, are you?' he said at once. 'I mean, you're not going to jump me and steal my cash, are you?'

Not criminals? We are now, I thought, remembering the boy we'd left unconscious at Perth Station, and the stolen car.

'Come on, let's push this car round the back of the garage and get that Granda of yours into the warm. I don't like the look of him.'

For the first time, I noticed Granda's pallor, the blue of his lips, his laboured breathing.

'He's cold,' I told the man, and I felt my granda's hands. They felt like frozen wax. 'I knew he was too cold.'

Together we pushed the car until it was hidden from view and then I tried to wake my granda to get him out. His eyes flickered open. He didn't know where he was, I could see that. The memory of the thug, stealing the car, driving those country roads, was gone for the moment. He began to panic, and when he caught sight of the ruddy-faced stranger who was bundling him out of the car he began to swear.

'Hey, Granda, watch your language. You'll be giving us two a bad name.'

He grabbed at me. 'Rory, what's going on? Who is he?'

I quietened him with soothing words. 'He's going to help us, Granda. He's a nice man.'

Yet, as the man almost carried my granda up the dark stairway to his flat above the garage, I realized I didn't have any real proof of that. He was a stranger, and I remembered then all the warnings my granda had always given me about never going with a stranger. This man's pleasant smile might mask all sorts of horrors.

Still, what choice did I have? My granda was so cold, so hungry. I didn't know how else to help him, except to trust this stranger.

The living room looked out on to the forecourt of the garage and it was bright and warm. Books and car magazines were piled up everywhere. A gas fire that looked just as if it were coal blazed in the hearth, and the man ('Just call me Rab,' he said) eased my granda gently into a big armchair.

'Something hot first, I think,' he said. 'Soup? Tea?'

Granda managed a pale smile. He hadn't heard a word, but he recognized the tone, kindness and concern.

'I'll switch on the TV,' Rab said. 'Might be something about you two on it.'

That thought made me panic. If Rab found out we were a couple of vicious thugs he might not be so eager to help.

Anyway, at first I couldn't concentrate on the television. It was my granda I was more interested in. His burst of energy, hot-wiring a car, driving all the way here, had taken so much out of him. Too much. He looked as if he had shrunk inside his clothes. He was so pale, and his hands? They were blue-white and couldn't stop shaking.

'Are you all right, Granda?' I asked him.

He read my lips. 'As long as I'm with you,' he said softly. Then his eyes closed, and he sank into sleep.

That was worrying. Not one of his cheeky replies, but a cheesy one. He really was ill. If only we were somewhere safe, somewhere we could stay forever. Maybe we *should* have moved up north, crossed to one of the islands, an uninhabited one. Lived off the land, like Robinson Crusoe and his Man Friday. Or stowed away on one of the cruise ships that called at Ocean Terminal and was bound for New York or the

Caribbean. Instead, I had dragged him to a caravan park.

I'd done all the wrong things. Made all the wrong decisions.

Nice one, Rory.

And now my granda looked done in, thanks to me.

If only I wasn't alone. If only there was someone to help me. I closed my eyes and sent another prayer up.

'OK, Big Man, I need some help here. I can't do this on my own.'

It was then that my ears caught the television reporter talking about us.

She was young, walking in the hills towards the camera, and my own home town lay spread out behind her.

'There is still no real sign of Rory and his grandfather, although sightings abound from Land's End to John o'Groats. The question is how could an old man and a boy disappear like this? The answer has to be that people are helping them. The public are very much on their side.'

It then cut to interviews with members of the public.

A woman clutching a toddler in her arms. 'I'd certainly help them. I think it's shameful going after them as if they were murderers.'

A man on his way to work. 'All the money in this country and there's no one to take these two in. It's a revolution we need. Things need changing!'

It went back to the reporter.

'In spite of all this support, the authorities are pleading with them to return. Their case will be looked into. Everything will be done to keep them together.'

Everything will be done, I thought. I bet. As soon as we gave ourselves up it would be back to Castle Street and Rachnadar, until they 'looked into it'.

The reporter was still talking.

'Mister McIntosh's son has been traced to Liverpool. There had been hope that they would make their way there, although the family has been estranged since Rory's birth. However, the son has heard nothing from them either.'

Can your heart stop beating for minutes? It must, because mine did then.

The Big Man works quickly sometimes.

I wasn't alone. Neither was my granda.

I had a dad.

He had a son.

And it was time he lived up to his responsibilities.

27

*R*ab came back into the living room carrying two mugs of tea. 'How about a sausage buttie?'

A sausage buttie. I suddenly realized just how hungry I was.

Rab nodded to the television. 'I thought you didn't have any family. And you've got a dad?'

He said it in that 'don't believe it' kind of way. I knew what he was thinking. This boy has a father, and he's on the run, alone, with this old man. Some father he must be.

I was thinking the same thing.

'What does your grandfather think about it?'

I shot a quick glance at my granda, still sleeping. 'Don't mention my dad to my granda. He goes berserk when you talk about him.'

How could I explain to anyone how my granda felt? How I felt? I realized then that I couldn't let on to my granda what I was planning, because since I'd heard the news a plan *was* forming in my mind.

Me and my granda were going to Liverpool. It was a port, there were boats there. We would go to Liverpool and make *him*, my dad, give us money. I didn't care how he got it. He could rob a bank for all I cared. (He probably had already. If he was rotten enough to just walk out of our lives then he was capable of anything!) He was still going to help us. It was about time. He had done nothing for me in his whole useless life . . . well, now was a good time to start.

The news on the other channel was coming on in half an hour and I wondered how I was going to listen without my granda hearing it too. In the end, nothing could have been easier. After waking up briefly and munching his buttie, Granda was so done in he allowed himself to be led into the bedroom. I only took off his shoes and covered him with a quilt and he was asleep in seconds.

Rab stood with me, watching him closely. 'You wouldn't let me get a doctor for him?'

That worried me. 'You won't turn us in, will you?'

'I won't turn you in, Rory.'

He cut me a big slice of chocolate fudge cake while we listened to the news bulletin. Now we had made the national news, and I watched open-mouthed as they reported people who had spotted us in supermarkets, begging on the street, at airports, everywhere. There had even been sightings of us in France.

'We sound like UFOs,' I said to Rab.

Then there were arguments and discussions about how the system had let us down, and how it was all society's fault. The break down of community, of family, the failure of social workers, everyone was blamed.

I wanted to scream at them all because I knew whose fault it all was. My dad's.

I stopped eating when his name was mentioned.

Jeff McIntosh. Granda hardly spoke his name, but I knew he too had been called after a film star. I didn't know which one.

'Neither Rory nor his grandfather have attempted to contact Jeff McIntosh in Liverpool.'

No mention of how he would welcome us with open arms if we did. He was probably already packing his suitcase to move on into oblivion once more, away from us. Too late, pal, I thought, I'm coming to get you.

As the story moved on, I realized that Rab was watching me intently. 'You're going there, aren't you?'

I wiped chocolate from my mouth and began to lie. 'No. Not interested in him.'

Rab was shaking his head. 'I'd go there if I was you. Let him take some responsibility for a change.'

My mind was doing loops. How would I find him? What did he look like?

It was as if Rab had heard my thoughts. 'You've brought your grandfather this far, Rory. You can take him to Liverpool. You'll find your father. He'll probably be in the phone book.'

The phone book! Of course. I felt better that night as I lay beside my granda. I could hear the wheezing deep inside his chest; unhealthy, painful wheezing. I would take him to Liverpool. I hadn't a clue how I would keep our destination from him, but I would have to try.

Rab was a good man. He had said he would help us.

Even so, I still wedged a chair under the door handle before I went to sleep. Nice man or not, who knew? By night he might turn into a werewolf, or a serial killer.

There was no point taking chances.

Granda fell out of bed during the night.

How he managed it I will never know. I mean, I was right beside him. He must have just rolled over and out he went. I thought the noise would have woken Rab but it didn't. I jumped out of bed too, got the fright of my life.

My granda was in a panic. He didn't know where he was. For a moment there was a terrifying realization that he didn't even recognize me!

'Where am I? Get me out of here! Who are you?'

Even in the dim light I could see fear in his watery, blue eyes. He was confused. The hot-wiring master criminal had disappeared. The shutters had come down again.

I helped him back into bed. 'Granda, we're safe. Go to sleep. I'm here. I'll watch you.'

'Oh, Rory, Rory,' he kept muttering. 'What have I come to?'

I didn't sleep for hours that night. I lay staring at the ceiling and I just got angrier and angrier.

My granda was done in, and we couldn't stop running. There was still a way to go. But at least now I knew where we were going.

We were going to Liverpool.

28

*I*t was early when I woke up, and the first thing I heard was Rab's low voice on the phone in the hall. I crept out of bed and listened at the door. What if he was phoning the police? His voice was just a murmur, but I could imagine him telling them to come and get us while we were still sleeping. Should I wake my granda up and get him ready so we could sneak out of the window?

Ha! That was a joke. Granda sneak anywhere. And we were on the first floor. Could he shimmy down the drainpipe? The mind boggled at the thought of it. No. The best thing to do, I decided, was confront Rab.

'Who were you phoning?' I asked him as soon as I went into his kitchen. He was making tea.

He looked at me and smiled. 'Mornin'. How did you sleep?'

'Never mind how I slept, who were you phoning?'

'Keep your shirt on. It wasn't the cops if that's what you're thinkin'.' He must have seen the relief on my face. 'That is what you thought, isn't it?' He handed me a cup of tea. 'Sit down, Rory. I've got a plan. I want to tell you all about it before your grandfather wakes up.'

He sat down across from me. 'I wish you could stay here, son. But I've got mates that pop in and out here all the time. Tonight they're coming to play cards. They're a good bunch, but they wouldn't be able to keep their mouths shut about you.'

'I know, we've got to go.' And I did know that, but I had hoped to stay there, sleeping warm and comfortable for even a few days more, till my granda got some strength back. 'What's your plan?'

'This morning I'm going to drive you down to the Borders.'

'You don't need to drive us anywhere. We've got a car.' Admittedly, it wasn't our car, but somehow that didn't matter at the moment.

'No, Rory, the cops are looking for that car. It was on the news this morning. And there was some young thug who says your Granda assaulted him.'

Panic flooded through me. Rab leaned across. 'Don't worry too much, Rory. Nobody believes him. That little rat is the one who looks like a thug, and he's claiming your grandfather knocked him out.' He shook his head. 'Aye, that poor ill old man. As if anybody is going to believe that!'

I tried not to grin.

Rab went on. 'So I'm going to drive you, and at the Borders we're going to meet up with my girlfriend, Annie.'

'You've told your girlfriend about us?'

'You can trust Annie. I can twist Annie round my little finger.'

What choice did I have? He trusted Annie, and I had to trust him.

'I can't understand why you're helping us.' And I didn't. We were strangers who had called into his garage for petrol in a stolen car.

Rab shrugged his shoulders. 'I feel the way so many people feel that have heard about you. Why should you not be together? There's got to be something we can do to make that possible. And I think now . . .' He paused. 'I think you know what that something might be. You know where you're going, don't you?'

Yes, I knew where I was going.

Rab nodded. 'We're all going to get you there, then.'

'We?'

He grinned. He looked just like one of my mates who had just scored a vital goal for the team. 'That's what I was on the phone arranging. A whole line of people who are going to take you to Liverpool.'

Rab helped me with my granda; helped get him dressed and shaved.

While I gave him his medicine, my granda said, 'People are kind, Rory. I thought the whole world was going to the dogs, and then you meet kindness like this. It's a wonderful world, Rory.'

A wonderful world. Here, in Rab, we had found another stranger who had helped, who had arranged a line of people who would take us to Liverpool. Passing us like the baton in a relay race. People who didn't even know us, but who were willing to help anyway.

'Where are we going now?' My granda asked as we got into Rab's truck.

'We're going with Rab, Granda.' I hoped he didn't ask anything else. He didn't. He just nodded, relying on me to keep him safe, to lead him. Me? It was unbelievable.

Rab drove for almost two hours while my granda snoozed in the back seat. We passed signs leading us further south on country roads with dips and bends and breathtaking scenery.

Finally, he pulled into a lay-by on a deserted stretch of road. Deserted, except for a woman who was standing beside a green car. She was chewing gum, and her red hair was tied up in a ponytail, although, between you and me, she looked too old for the chewing gum or the ponytail. She was also wearing jeans that looked two sizes too small.

Rab leapt from the truck and they ran to each other enthusiastically. He began kissing her passionately . . . or should I say eating her. It was disgusting. It made me feel like throwing up.

It didn't have that effect on my granda. He came to in the back just in time to see the performance. 'Aw, that's lovely.'

'Lovely? It's disgusting, Granda. And in a public place. In front of children! It shouldn't be allowed. Adults have some really disgusting habits!'

'Och, you wait till you're eighteen, you'll be kissing lassies left right and centre.'

I was beginning to feel like throwing up again. 'I

don't think. I'd have to be under anaesthetic.'

That only made him laugh, and when Rab had finally finished eating Annie they both came across to the truck, arms entwined. I noticed she was still chewing her gum.

'So, these are the fugitives, eh?' She leaned her head in the window and grinned. Of course, she won my granda over with her red hair. He just can't resist redheads. Even brightly dyed ones like Annie.

He grinned right back at her. 'So are you going to help us too, darling?' he asked her.

'Sure am. But first you're going to eat.' She tickled Rab in the ribs. 'Got to keep my man well fed, eh?' Rab giggled like someone really daft. And I'd thought he was sensible! 'My big man likes his food.'

Annie had brought flasks of soup and tea, crusty bread and fruit. It was delicious. I could tell my granda was enjoying it too. He kept spluttering crumbs all over the place.

Rab left after we'd eaten our fill. I didn't know how to thank him, and he didn't want me to. 'This is the best fun I've had in ages, and it let me see my darlin' Annie.'

Of course, he had to eat her again before he left, and she still didn't take her chewing gum out of her mouth.

Finally, she herded us into her green car and switched on the engine.

'Right! Who's for some music?' The radio blared out and who was singing, but Frank Sinatra.

Granda burst into song along with him, and so did Annie.

I sighed and leaned back in the seat. Nothing I could do about it. It was fate.

29

'WELCOME TO ENGLAND' the sign proclaimed. We were heading south, closer and closer to Liverpool.

My granda noticed the sign too, mainly because Annie pointed it out to him.

'Where are we going?'

I thought about my answer. He hadn't seen the news. As far as I knew he wasn't aware where his son was living now. It would be easier to tell him the truth. 'Liverpool.'

'Liverpool?' He sounded surprised, as if I'd suggested the moon as our destination.

'Aye, Liverpool. I thought we might get a boat there. Stowaway. That would be exciting.'

Granda wasn't as daft as he looked sometimes. 'We could have done that back home. What are we going to Liverpool for?'

'The scenery,' I said.

He mumbled on, moaning about what a waste of time this was, and us giving these good people all this trouble. 'To go to Liverpool!' he said again.

'Yes, Liverpool. And if you've got a better idea you can go yourself.'

Annie glanced at me, still chewing away. Then she

glanced at my granda. 'Want me to stop? You could hitch a lift back.'

'I've got a good mind to do just that. Liverpool indeed!'

Annie said in a whisper. 'I take it he doesn't know?'

Why is it my granda's ears always work at the wrong times? He heard that perfectly. 'Don't know what?'

Annie covered up with panache. 'Don't know I can't take you all the way to Liverpool.'

Granda sat up straight. 'So, where are we going now?'

'To my cousin in the Lake District. She'll drive you on from there. But you can get a good night's sleep at her place. She lives in this lovely remote cottage. Her husband's got a brilliant job. They're absolutely loaded.'

Granda leaned forward and grinned at her. 'You're taking an awful risk helping us. You could be shot for what you're doing.'

'No, Granda,' I reminded him. 'We are not prisoners of war on the run. This is not a war film. Nobody's going to get shot.'

He punched my shoulder. 'Well, you might, boy, if you keep talking to me like that.'

Meanwhile, Annie had started reminiscing fondly about her cannibal boyfriend. 'See my Rab. Life's just a thrill a minute with him. You never know what he's going to do next. He phones me up and tells me all about how we're going to help you two. He gets it all organized, a chain of people taking you to safety.' I was beginning to think she was as daft as my granda. Her next words confirmed this. She turned right round to him and smiled. 'You're right, Granda, it is like an escape in a war movie – and I'm a beautiful member of the French Resistance.'

I let out a yell. She was wobbling all over the road. 'Eyes front!'

She giggled. 'Sorry.'

How could I blame her? Whatever was wrong with my granda, she had obviously caught it. Life is not like a movie. I wanted to tell her.

We pulled into the drive of her cousin's remote cottage just as dusk was falling. A woman came hurrying out of the front door. I had expected a dead ringer for Annie, but, instead, the woman looked quite glamorous. Blonde hair and tight, black trousers, and she wasn't bulging out of them the way Annie was.

'You're gorgeous,' was the first thing my granda said to her. I felt like melting into the ground . . . again.

She smiled, and looked even more glamorous. 'Oh, a charmer, are you?' She slipped an arm into his and helped him out of Annie's car. 'Let's get inside. It's going to be a really cold night'.

It already was. The dusk was bringing with it a frost into the clear, blue night.

'My name's Norma,' she said as soon as we were inside the front door. Her house was so cosy. There was a big blazing fire in the hearth, and this time it really did look real, not gas, and there were big floral chairs you could get lost in. My granda sank into one with a sigh, and in the firelight I could see how tired he really was.

'I've made some dinner for you.' Norma bent down to Granda. 'Do you like steak pie?'

'Oh lovely, sweetheart,' he said. But I knew he hadn't really heard her. He was, like me, overcome by these people's kindness.

'This is my daughter, Nicola.' Nicola's head appeared from round one of the chairs. She waved a greeting. And then disappeared again.

Her mother tutted. 'Don't just sit there. Come over and make friends.'

Nicola got up reluctantly. Obviously her favourite TV programme was on. She came across and stared at me. 'You're on the telly every night. You look better on the telly.'

I ignored that. Didn't believe it anyway. 'You can get my autograph later,' I said, cheekily.

'That's a good idea. I can sell it, and make a fortune.'

Nicola looked just like her mother, except for the blonde hair. She was dark.

'I think it's terrible the way they're after you. I think it's great what you've done.'

My granda heard that all right. He grinned stupidly and ruffled my hair. 'He's a great boy, my Rory.'

After we had freshened up . . . and Granda had used the toilet – those bowels again (I was dead embarrassed when he came back and told everyone about it, but Annie almost fell off her seat laughing) – we sat in the big country kitchen and ate the steak pie and the mashed potatoes that Norma had made for us, finishing it off with ice cream. It was the best meal I'd ever tasted.

Annie left soon after that, still chewing. She left my granda as if she were his favourite daughter. Hugging him, crying and promising always to keep in touch. She really did think she was in a movie.

When she'd gone, Norma insisted that Granda go to bed. 'You look done in. And we've got a busy day tomorrow. I wish you could stay longer, but my husband will be back and I don't think he'd approve of this.' She sounded as if she wasn't so sure either.

'It's good of you to drive us to Liverpool,' I said. 'Once we're there, we'll be fine.'

My granda was shaking his head. 'I don't understand why we're going there?'

Norma glanced at me and I shook my head frantically.

Her brows furrowed. 'Just you sit there, Mister McIntosh and I'll bring you in a cup of tea.'

'Make it a mug,' my granda told her.

She pulled me into the kitchen with her. 'Don't you think you should tell him, Rory? He has a right to know that you're taking him to his son.'

Obviously, Annie had told her.

But I had no doubt what my granda's reaction would be to that. 'You don't know what he is like, Norma. He'll hardly mention his name. Says he hasn't got a son any more.'

'So what are you going to do when you find him?' Nicola asked.

I shrugged. 'I don't know. I'm making this up as I go along.'

Norma looked worried. 'You've taken on too much, Rory. He's an old man. He doesn't look well.'

'He's my granda,' was all I said. Because in the end there was no other answer. He was my granda, and he was relying on me.

At that moment there was an almighty roar from the living room. I jumped to my feet, sure my granda was having a heart attack. Nicola and Norma rushed into the living room with me, and my granda was on his feet too, unsteadily and with a face red with rage. He was going crazy, pointing at the television screen.

I caught my breath. It was that photograph of us, behind the reporter. I could hardly hear what she was saying, but her words were subtitled on the screen.

'The police are sure that the pair will eventually make their way to Liverpool where Mister McIntosh's son, Jeff, now lives.'

My granda yelled so loudly I felt my ears shiver. 'So that's why we're going to Liverpool!'

30

*S*o, now he knew and he didn't like it. Not one bit. 'You think I'm going to him?' He was growing frantic, spittle forming on his mouth. His whole body was shaking. 'I am not going to Liverpool. Do you hear me?'

I looked at Norma and Nicola. Norma lifted her shoulders and shrugged, but Nicola was nodding. I knew she understood how I felt better than her mother. Granda was being unreasonable, I knew that. I could have cried with frustration. I had thought I had it all figured out. Go to Liverpool. Let my granda's son, my father, deal with it. But now that my granda knew my plan there was no way he would go there.

In the end, I quietened him by assuring him that I'd do anything he wanted. We wouldn't go to him. We would go east, to Hull maybe, catch a boat to Holland from there.

'Promise me, Rory.' My granda's eyes were brimming with tears. 'It would hurt you too much if he just turned his back on you now.' But what I really think he meant was that it would hurt him too much.

I promised, over and over again. And the more I promised the more I hated that dad of mine. His name was constantly mentioned on the television, but never once had he appeared. Never once had he looked into the camera and said, 'Come to me. I'm here. I'll help.' Granda was right. He didn't want us there at all. The media or the police had found him, hounded him, but he wanted nothing to do with his doddery old father, or me, the son he hadn't seen since I was a baby.

I went to bed that night hating someone. Hating this man who was my granda's son, and my father.

I couldn't wake my granda the next morning. Yesterday had taken too much out of him. Now he was in such a deep sleep, wheezing noisily, his face like wax.

I ran for Norma, dragged her in to look at him. 'Do you think he's all right?'

She looked concerned. Genuinely concerned. She felt his brow, the pulse at his neck. 'I don't think you can go anywhere today,' she said.

'But your husband, he's coming back.'

She waved that away. 'He's not back till late tonight.' Norma bit her lip thoughtfully. 'Let your granda rest just now. I've got to go into town. We'll see how he is when I come back.'

Nicola wanted to stay with me, but her mum refused. 'I'm going in to visit your gran. She knows I'd never leave you here on your own. Too many questions if you don't come, Nicola.'

Nicola still didn't want to go. She was worried about my granda too. 'Will you phone me, if there's any problem?' She quickly gave me her mobile phone number.

'If you see this number come up on the caller display, you'll know it's an emergency. I've found out something. And if you need to phone me . . .' She left that hanging in the air. I knew what she meant and it scared me. If my granda died. If he stopped breathing altogether.

I grinned. 'Nothing's going to kill my granda.'

But after they'd gone I wondered if that was true. I sat beside him and his every breath seemed to pain him.

I counted out his pills as I waited. How long would they last? How many days? And how would I get some more? Problems seemed to be piling up all around me.

He woke up in the early afternoon, completely disorientated. He began thrashing about wildly as if I was about to put handcuffs on him.

'I was dreaming,' he explained at last. 'Dreamin' they were after us. They'd caught us, and we had to run. We never stopped running.'

I got him out of bed. I had to get him dressed, no matter how tired he was. Later, when Norma came back, we would have to go, to move on. Never stop running. I was exhausted at the thought of it.

While I made tea I left him sitting on the sofa watching television. Unfortunately it was a talk show about ungrateful children. Just the right thing for him to watch! I ran from the kitchen when I heard him shouting back at the television.

'They're useless! You work all your life for them and they turn their back on you. You wish they'd never been born.'

He was getting excited again and I calmed him down.

'I take that back, son. I don't wish he'd never been born. I wouldn't have you, if I hadn't had him.'

'Why do you hate him so much, Granda?'

'I don't *hate* him,' he said, but he lied. 'He's just a worthless piece of nothing. Not worth bothering about. We've never needed him, and we don't need him now.'

The afternoon wore on and still Norma and Nicola didn't return. Granda fell asleep again along the sofa, but I kept watching the clock. We would have to leave tonight, before Norma's husband came back. It would be a long, tiring drive for my granda. What was keeping them?

Icy dusk was falling when the phone rang. Granda didn't hear it. I held my breath as I approached the phone. There was no way I was going to answer it unless . . . unless it was Nicola's mobile number. Emergency.

I read the number on caller display and my heart turned to stone. Nicola's number.

I grabbed at the phone, answered breathlessly. 'Nicola?'

She was almost in tears. I could hear it in her voice. 'Oh, Rory. My mum's told on you. She's been to the police. They're coming to get you. You've got to get out of there . . . Now!'

31

Nicola kept babbling on. 'She didn't mean anything bad. She's just worried about your granda. She says he can't take any more of this running away. And it's too much for you too. She doesn't understand, Rory. I tried to stop her. Honest, I did.'

I was hardly listening. It didn't matter why she'd done it. She'd done it.

I stood staring at my granda, his hair tousled, his teeth still in a glass by the bed. How long would it take me to get him ready to go? How long did I have? And most importantly, where were we going to go?

'When will they be here?'

There were still tears in her voice. 'Anytime. They were waiting for someone, probably the FBI, or something. She doesn't know I'm phoning.' Suddenly she gasped. 'She's coming, Rory. I've got to go. Good luck.'

Granda's shoes were toasting by the fire and, as I slipped them on his feet, he woke up.

'Are we going?' he asked.

I shrugged an answer. 'We've got to.'

He didn't hear me. His hearing aid was lying by the bed too.

He grabbed at my jumper. 'Not Liverpool.' It was an order, not a question.

'Not Liverpool, Granda.' Liverpool was out of the question now. Probably a daft idea to begin with.

I shoved as much as I could into my rucksack, including some bread and crisps. It wasn't stealing. Norma would understand. I tried to be angry with her, but I couldn't. She hadn't meant us harm. She just didn't understand that I would never be parted from my granda for anything.

All the while I got things ready, I was thinking about where we should go. Not on to the main road, certainly. The police would probably arrive that way. No, we would take the remote back roads, quiet and deserted. I imagined us finding a shack there, resting till morning, moving on fresh.

My granda stood by the door, like a puppy waiting for me to take him out for a walk.

I smiled at him. 'C'mon, Granda, it's the Great Escape once again.'

Was I glad I took the back road! As we climbed the hill behind the house I could see the lights of two police cars wind their way along the main road heading for Norma's isolated cottage.

The hill took a lot out of my granda. He was wheezing even worse, and I realized with an awful lurch in my stomach that I'd forgotten to bring his teeth. I could imagine the police finding them, staring up at them from the glass by the bed.

When we got to the top of the hill I made him sit down on a tree trunk. But he could only rest for a moment, because I knew when the police reached the house and found we had gone, they would be searching all through these hills, all the back roads, knowing we couldn't have gone far.

'Are you ready, Granda?' It was a stupid question. Of course, he wasn't ready. He was exhausted. Yet he stood up unsteadily, right away.

'Ready for anything, son,' he said.

We stumbled on in the darkness eventually hitting a road, with the icy cold seeping into our bones. I had to watch Granda carefully, in case he slipped on the frosty surface. All the while I listened for a police car wailing towards us or, more likely, purring silently, like a tiger stalking its prey.

But there was nothing. Not one solitary car came along that moonlit road. It was as if we were in another world. How I wished we were.

The stars were clear and bright. Granda for all his tiredness began pointing them out to me.

'That's Orion,' he said with a wheeze, 'and see that one there, that's Andromeda.'

'Since when did you become Patrick Moore?' I asked him. 'The nearest you ever get to the stars is watching *Star Trek*.'

'You don't know half of what I know, boy,' he answered me. 'A fount of information. A blinkin' encyclopaedia, that's me.'

'What a load of twaddle you talk, old man.'

That's how we walked along that road, arguing as usual.

But Granda walked slower with every shuffling step and his breathing grew worse.

I was growing more worried about him by the second.

Suddenly, I heard it in the distance. A car. Some instinct told me it wasn't any old car. It was a police car.

I gave my granda a shove. 'Run, Granda. Across the road, through that hedge.'

He ran. Oh, how he ran. As if the Gestapo itself were after him. Not wanting to be caught. I wanted desperately to have the strength to lift him, to carry him.

I could hear the car come closer. Any second now it would round the bend in the road and see us.

'Faster!' I said softly.

He heard that too. He put on a spurt, like an athlete heading for the finishing line, almost threw himself at the hedge, just a moment before I did. We rolled in the ditch and lay flat, just as the car turned the corner, and moved quietly past us. Watching for us. A second earlier, and they would have seen us.

I waited until it had disappeared before I asked, 'Are you OK, Granda?' I tugged at his sleeve and he turned his face to me. Too white. His voice too tired.

'Me?' He had hardly any breath left. 'Fine.'

But he was far from fine.

I peeked above the ditch. In the distance I could see what looked like a stone bus shelter. He needed to rest. This would have to do.

I pulled him to his feet and we set off towards the shelter. He stumbled and I did my best to keep him upright. There was a bench inside and Granda sank on to it gratefully. 'A bit of a sit-down for a minute, that's all I need.'

'Are you hungry, Granda?'

That set him off laughing. 'I'm starving. But I haven't got any teeth. Remember?'

I pretended to pull out mine. 'Here, have a loan of these.'

'You cheeky devil. You might have brought me something soft.'

'Like a mattress?'

He let out a long, heavenly sigh. 'Oh, what a lovely thought.' He was picturing a big fluffy mattress, imaging himself sinking into it.

He closed his eyes, and his face was so drawn and so pale it worried me even more. 'Maybe we should go back, Granda. You need to sleep on a mattress, in a bed. Maybe they would let us stay together now.'

My granda's eyes snapped open. 'No, Rory. Nothing's changed. I'd rather be here in this cold bus shelter with you than anywhere else in the world. I want us to stay together as long as we can. Is it a deal?'

'It's a deal, Granda.'

He nodded, contented with my answer. 'You know, if I die tonight, I'll die a happy man.'

'Don't say that, Granda!' I shouted at him.

He laughed again. 'Don't worry. I've not got any

intention of dying, son. I want this film to have a happy ending.'

He chuckled as he laid himself along the bench. 'I'll just shut my eyes for five minutes. Eh? You can be the lookout. I'll take the second watch.'

There he went again, talking as if we were in a movie.

I put my rucksack under his head as a pillow and within minutes of closing his watery eyes he was snoring like a bear. I would give him fifteen minutes, I thought, as I watched along the deserted road, and then we would have to move on. Time enough for him to get a little rest. I sat beside him and prayed.

'Come on, Big Man. Help me. Tell me where I should go next?'

I can't remember falling asleep but I did. I don't even know how long I slept. I jumped awake into a silent night. Not a bird. Not a rustle of trees or bushes. There wasn't a breath of wind.

Granda wasn't even snoring any more. I stood up and stretched. Time to wake him, I thought. We would have some cheese and bread . . . but of course, he couldn't eat that, not without his teeth! How could I have forgotten them? For a moment the problems stretched ahead of me like an obstacle course. But I shrugged them away. We were still here, we hadn't been caught. There was still hope.

I laid a hand on my granda's shoulder to wake him, and a cold shiver ran through me, as if someone had just walked over my grave. His colour was all wrong. In fact, he didn't have any colour at all. His skin was like the wax fruit you see in bowls in furniture shops. His mouth was hanging open.

He wasn't snoring.

He wasn't breathing.

My granda was dead.

32

I screamed at him. 'Granda!' Wanting desperately to shock him back to life. But he didn't stir. I took a step out of the shelter and looked up and down the moonlit road, wishing, praying for someone to come along.

'Granda!' I yelled again, and this time I wanted someone to hear my voice as it echoed over the hills.

He lay still. Dead? No!

Then I began to run. Didn't know where I was going. Didn't care. Looking for someone to help my granda, because he couldn't be dead. I couldn't let that happen. Grandas like mine didn't die. And if he was . . . it would be all my fault anyway. Stealing him away. Dragging him from one place to another, never resting properly. I ran and the only sound on that road was my shoes clattering in panic.

I don't know how long I was running until I finally saw a house, set back from the road. It was in darkness, everyone asleep, a big Range Rover parked in the driveway.

I was yelling even before I reached the front door. 'Help! Please! Somebody help me!'

As I pounded on the door, a dog began to bark excitedly, but it seemed an age before a light was switched on in an upstairs window. A curtain was drawn back and I took a step away from the house and called up. 'Help! Please!'

It was only then I realized I was crying.

The front door opened just a moment later. A big man in a dressing gown was holding a growling Alsatian by the collar. Behind him on the stairs a woman peeked anxiously.

'My granda,' I was almost sobbing. 'Please help my granda. I think he's dead.'

The woman stepped closer. 'William, it's the boy we've been hearing about on the news.' She looked at me. 'You're Rory, aren't you?'

She said my name as if I was someone she knew well, and she smiled.

'Rory,' the man repeated. 'Come on, where's this granda of yours.' He turned to the woman. 'Alice, phone the police. As soon as I know where he is I'll get in touch on the mobile.'

He disappeared back into the house for just a second, then we were in his car and we were roaring off back along the road.

My whole body was shaking as we drove that road, and my thoughts just a panicked jumble. But one thought kept surfacing: it was over. They hadn't caught us, no. But I had gone to them. Because I had no choice. Ruby's words had come true.

And I remembered her other words: *a terrible sadness*. Had that also come true?

I kept praying that when the bus shelter came into

view again my granda would be standing there, waiting for me, brandishing his fist in fury at being deserted in the middle of the night.

Not dead at all.

But he wasn't.

In fact, it was worse. While I'd been gone he had fallen off the bench and now he lay, face down, with his arm twisted beneath him. I wanted to lift him, hug him, but the man held me back.

'You go and sit in the car, Rory. I'll get an ambulance here.'

'Is he dead?' I asked, but he didn't answer me.

He only said again. 'You go and sit in the car.'

After that everything was a blur. The police cars arrived, two of them. So did the ambulance. Someone put a blanket round my shoulders, someone pushed a mug of hot tea into my hands and guided me into one of the police cars. Someone asked me questions I didn't listen to, didn't want to answer. When my granda's body was stretchered into the ambulance I looked at the policewoman in the front seat and asked her, 'Can I go with him? I'm not leaving him on his own.'

She smiled. 'We'll follow in a minute. I promise. But first, there's someone who wants to talk to you.'

Couldn't they see I didn't want to talk to anyone? Not then.

'I'm going with my granda!' I said angrily.

The policewoman had the decency to look embarrassed. So did the man who came towards me. No uniform, a plain-clothes policeman obviously.

He got in the car beside me.

'They're not going to separate us now!' I told him.

'Don't worry. You're going with him. We both are.'

'You as well? You think he's going to make a break for it!' My voice cracked. 'I don't think he's fit for that any more.'

The man's face was pale, full of concern. He's trying to tell me something, I thought. I knew he was. I thought I knew already what that something was. My granda really was dead. They couldn't save him. I'd left him alone too long.

'What are you trying to say? Just tell me!' I yelled it so loud the policemen by the bus shelter turned to look at me.

The man beside me looked deep into my eyes. But when he did speak, it wasn't what I was expecting at all.

'Rory, I'm your dad,' he said.

33

I know what you're thinking. Big deathbed scene. Reconciliation. Granda fading fast, and his son on his knees by his bedside, begging forgiveness. A nurse in a corner drying her tears on her apron. And just before he slips his mortal coil . . . my granda reaches out his hand, touches his son's head, and forgives him.

Ha! Scrap that notion.

My granda isn't dead.

I'm going to have to shoot the old codger.

Oh, it was touch and go for a while. He lay for days, hovering between life and death. I wanted to stay there with him and, for the first couple of nights, I did. But then, I met his family, my dad's family. Mine too, I suppose. And they insisted I come home with them.

His wife, Karen, is small and pretty and quiet. It must have been something of a shock for her to discover her husband had a son, and a father he'd never mentioned before. But she seems to have come to terms with it quite well. She asked me to come and stay with them while my granda was in hospital. And as soon as I knew he was going to survive, that's what I did.

I've got two little sisters as well.

Horrors.

One of them is Rhonda. She's five and just wants to hold your hand and kiss you. She's bad, but the other, Ava, is only three and I'm already seriously worried about her. The first time she came in to my granda's room in the hospital, she climbed on his bed and got her head stuck in the bars. That's what brought him back to consciousness actually, her screaming. She was the first thing he saw when he opened his eyes. This toddler, bawling her lungs out, with her head stuck in the bedrails. It's a wonder he didn't have a relapse.

Needless to say, he fell in love with both of them right away. He lets them climb all over him, and kiss him and play with his hearing aid until it whistles.

He likes Karen too. I can tell.

And my dad? My granda still treats him badly. Hardly talks to him, but Rhonda and Ava will bring him round eventually. My dad's all right, actually. OK, I admit I said some awful things about him, but that was before I got to know him. The trouble is, he just doesn't know how to handle my granda like I do. You've got to throw the insults right back at him, and my dad can't do that. Every time my granda insults him, he just keeps apologizing to him.

He's always apologizing to me too, making feeble excuses for deserting us.

'I was young, Rory, and stupid. Too scared to come back because my dad said he hated me. Didn't want to see me again. But as soon as I saw the two of you on the news, I got in touch with the police. Honest. Just give me a chance to prove I can be a good dad again, a good son.'

It turned out that he had been the 'someone' the police had been waiting for when Nicola had called that night. Not the FBI.

So, it looks as if we're staying in Liverpool. I suppose I'll get used to it, except everybody here thinks they're a comedian. Luckily, so does my granda. He loves it. The social workers have got a flat for me and him just round the corner from my dad and Karen. My dad comes every day and helps out, and we go to his place for our dinner and things. Now we've got home helps, and care workers and meals on wheels and there's even a tuck-in service that helps me to get my granda into bed at night. You name it, we've got it. Why couldn't they have done that for us before? But then, if they had, we would never have found my dad, my family.

Was that what Ruby meant? *I'd find what I was looking for?* Because now I know that's what I was looking for, though I didn't realize it. I know now that even when my granda does go, I won't ever be alone again. I'm lucky.

I think sometimes of the awful Tess, screaming her fear at everyone. Tess, scared of being alone. She's not so lucky.

I think of them all. Everyone who helped us on our journey.

Norma and Nicola. I've forgave Norma a long time

ago. She's a really nice person. She was worried about my granda, that's why she went to the police that day.

And Annie and Rab. We're going to their wedding in the summer.

And Ruby and Sammy and Tyrone. They're coming to visit us soon, and if anybody tells them to move on I'll throw my granda at them.

I miss Darren but his mum's invited us up to her caravan for a holiday as soon as my granda is well enough. We're looking forward to that. Darren's granny's coming over from Jamaica to visit as well. She drives Darren potty just the way my granda does me. She's got this loud laugh that sets your teeth on edge. If only she'd known, she says, she would have come over and taken care of my granda. Darren and me have always thought she fancied him. Funny thing is, I think he fancies her too. And she hasn't even got red hair!

Since my granda came back from the dead (because I am sure he did – my granda *was* dead in that shelter), his memory is even worse than before. I found him in the hall cupboard the other day, and when I opened the door, he said, 'Thank goodness you came, son. I've been stuck in this lift all morning.'

And the doctors say it will only get worse. They say too the damage that was done to his lungs is 'irreparable', I think that's the word.

But we're together. We'll always be together. And I've found a family.

So, is this a happy ending? I don't know. But it's good enough for me.

hotnews@puffin

Hot off the press!

You'll find all the latest exclusive Puffin news here

Where's it happening?

Check out our author tours and events programme

Bestsellers

What's hot and what's not? Find out in our charts

E-mail updates

Sign up to receive all the latest news
straight to your e-mail box

Links to the coolest sites

Get connected to all the best author web sites

Book of the Month

Check out our recommended reads

www.puffin.co.uk